THE FOUNDRY

REBUILDING HOPE
BOOK 4

P A WILSON

Ebook ISBN: 978-1-990509–30-8
Paperback ISBN: 978-1-990509–29-2
Audio book ISBN:978-1-990509–31-5

FREE EBOOK

Claim your copy of A Choice to Make when you sign up for my newsletter and get a glimpse of Lena and Brian at the end of the plagues.

1

——————

The farmhouse kitchen was warm from the ovens. The spring sun on the windows brightened the room. A lingering aroma of bread baking and bacon frying from breakfast all added to the feeling of home and safety.

Lena stood at the sink, watching Scott as he ran his finger along old roads on the map he'd laid out on the table. She loved his passion for exploring the world but hated that he was leaving for so long. This time would be a year at least.

"Tik thinks we should go south this time," Scott said. "Check out completely new territory."

"Would it be a shorter route?"

She knew she shouldn't agree just to get him back earlier, but it was hard. He'd taken so long to heal from his wound during the battle against Cole's men. Then he'd escorted the people who followed Poorjohn to a new home. She'd hoped he got the wanderlust out of his system, but no. Scott and Tik were determined to find out what was happening to what used to be the United States and

Canada. At least he wasn't thinking of going as far as what was left of Mexico, adding months to the journey.

Lena understood the need to know, and if they were ever going to pull a country out of the scattered communities, they would need to convince individual leaders. The only way to do that, since the technology and power grid failed, was to go on horseback, or foot.

"Distance, maybe. We'd avoid being caught by winter as we moved south, but the only thing we know about south is that the weather will be better."

Lena stepped to his side and looked at the map. South was where they'd come from. Not that upstate New York was considered the south, but all she had were bad memories of being in a city overrun by gangs. And the real south? Early news before everything went to shit was that generations of conspiracies about medical care left the population unable to fight off the mutated viruses. It meant hardly any people survived to build communities.

"What if it's empty? I mean, it's hard to survive alone. You need people around to protect you, people with different skills."

"It's been long enough that people could have moved in from all over." Scott ran his finger along the line of I-95. "It's a straight shot for people in New York City to get to anywhere along the coast."

"Big city people fending for themselves?" Lena thought of their first year on the farm. "I guess it could work. There are a lot of books about farming."

Scott put his arm around Lena and pulled her close. "I don't agree with Tik. We'll eventually have to go south, but I want to cross to the west coast."

It would mean hitting winter somewhere and being stuck for a couple of months, at least. Lena tried to think through the options. She wouldn't talk him into staying. Why did crossing the continent feel like a better choice? It's not like the area around what was the border between the US and Canada was a haven of like-minded people. But it did sit right with her.

"You could head through to Seattle or Portland," she said. "Then, in spring, you could head to California and then back. Go a little through Arizona and New Mexico."

"Why don't you come along?" Scott hugged her again. "I don't like the idea of leaving you here any more than you like me leaving."

"I'm needed here," she said. "I just wish we had a way to send and receive news. We need to set up some form of communication if unity is the goal."

"You're thinking way into the future," Scott said. "Do we really need to have a purpose more than having a look around?"

Yes.

"When you went last time, what kind of reception did you get?" She knew the stories but only as events to be shared around a campfire.

Scott pointed to the map and then traced the route. "We didn't go far, and we had a lot of people slowing us down."

"And you weren't trying to connect with communities," she added. "But now you are, and that's very different."

"Yeah, we'll go faster," he said. "But more sidetracks. I'm not sure how we'll find communities. I guess the answer to my question about purpose is yes. Now that I talk about it more, we are looking for signs of any threats coming our way."

Lena hadn't considered that aspect. Another community headed to the farm to destroy what she'd built with the local towns. Was that naive? Newton Cole saw the area as the best route to the west and attacked them, hoping to gain control. "What reason would anyone have to attack us?"

Scott looked up from the map. "There are plenty of reasons to take us, including just wanting to control everyone."

Lena put the kettle on the hot range for tea. Scott's question had changed something inside her. Fear turned to curiosity, or maybe she'd conceded the fight going on in her head. Scott was going, and she had to make the best of it. "I guess what I mean is, why would anyone in the west want to come this way?"

"Isn't that why we're going?" He pulled out a chair and sat. "Maybe someone thinks we're coping better than them. Maybe a conspiracy nut thinks we have power and computers and TV."

Lena laughed. "Would you want that? To have everything back?"

"It would be nice to have a tractor and a car, and a cellphone so I can text anyone I want to. But I wasn't much more than a kid before. I didn't understand the world, really. I like what we have here. I want to make sure we keep it."

"Yes, you're my boy toy." She poured tea for both of them and joined him at the table. "I like what we have, too. In the old world everything was easier, but not many people were satisfied."

"Then let's not bring back the old days. I'll settle the route details with Tik tomorrow. I want to be on the road in the next couple of weeks. With luck, we'll be on the coast before the weather turns."

2

————

Lena stood at the window looking over the fields. The ground was ready for planting; so much hope of seeds germinating in the next few weeks.

Her night had been disturbed with thoughts of the dangers Scott would be facing. He could die without her knowing. Both of them could. And she'd forever wonder if there was something she could have done or said to make him safe.

She'd only had two men in her life she could say she loved. Brian was her husband, and before the plague, she would have said she would be with him until the "death do you part" thing. He changed so much after that she couldn't wait to escape the life he offered.

Now she had Scott. At first, she resisted her feelings; he was so young. But as she got to know him, his youth simply didn't matter. Five years living on the road gave him far more experience of the world than she had.

She pulled on a cardigan to make up for the early spring chill and headed for the kitchen. People would be rising soon, and a good breakfast was important for hard physical work.

Mellow was placing loaves of dough in the oven, the aroma of bread baking already filling the room with comfort.

"What's next?" Lena asked.

"You aren't on kitchen duty this week," Mellow said as she set the timer. "You should enjoy a sleep in."

"If only," Lena said. "Should I start the bacon?"

"Sure. Do you want some tea?"

For a second, Lena craved coffee. There wasn't any. Maybe the exploration would go as far as California, where some rumors of coffee producers starting up gave people hope. But for now, tea was the only thing on offer. "Love some. How do you feel about Tik heading out?"

Mellow poured tea and sat, lifting her feet onto the chair opposite. "I'm trying to keep busy. Is that why you can't sleep?"

"Can you? I keep thinking about our trip here. We ran into more than our share of danger. And we were nine people. How are they going to manage with just two?"

"I keep thinking everything beyond what we're used to is filled with cannibals. Or people like Newton Cole who just want power over everyone."

Lena chuckled and turned the bacon over in the pan. "I think, by now, things have stabilized beyond the cannibals, but thanks for putting that in my head."

"Yeah, but Cole's sort is always around." Mellow finished her tea and went to the pantry to pull out the basket of eggs. "I'd be happier if Keith went with them."

The original plan was to take Jason, Ava's son, but the boy had his fill of camping on the road when he helped Poorjohn's people and Brian find a new community. "Keith won't leave Deb for that long." Lena envied Deb's ability to keep her husband close. "Plus, we'll need him while they're gone."

Mellow checked the timer. "Bread will be out in five minutes. I can hear people stirring upstairs."

"The bacon is done. Do we have anything else left in the storeroom to add?"

Mellow nodded toward two bowls sitting on the window ledge. "Some dried fruit and tomatoes. I set them to soften before I started the bread."

The rhythm of preparing a meal was like meditation. Lena didn't want to bring the topic of the men's trip back into the peace, but Mellow was the only person who understood what she was going through. And when everyone came for food, it would be a rush of eating and cleaning.

Lena put the bacon on a cloth-covered plate to drain and started to lay out plates and cutlery. "Has Tik asked you if you want to come with them?"

"No. I didn't even think of going."

"Scott asked me to come. I think he might have been joking."

Mellow pulled the bread out of the oven and placed the loaves on a cooling rack. Then she looked at Lena closely. "Did you consider it?"

Lena shook her head. She placed napkins on the table and started the kettle boiling for the large teapot. She hadn't considered it when he asked, but now it sounded more attractive. At least if Scott died on the road, she'd be with him, even if was just to die alongside him.

"Why not?" Mellow grabbed Lena's elbow to stop her fussing with the table setting. "Lena? What if we could make it work? Are you interested in seeing what's out there?"

"We need to get breakfast going," Lena said. She gently

pulled Mellow's fingers from her elbow. "I don't know what I want, but if you want to join the men, you need to tell Tik soon so you can be part of the planning."

Mellow touched one of the loaves. Ideally, they would rest longer before cutting, but that never happened, and it was rare to have any leftovers. Bread was baked twice a day since the flour mill opened in Crystal. She grabbed the bread knife and sawed the ends off the first loaf. "You need to make up your mind too, Lena. When we're gone, you won't have a chance of catching up."

3

Next year was on Lena's mind as she sipped iced tea on the porch after dinner. It could be that long before she sat here once more, looking out over her home. In an hour, as soon as the dining room and kitchen were cleared, Scott, Mellow, and Tik would join her. She was going to tell Scott that she was joining them on the journey. The four of them would plan out a path, and tomorrow, they would start the preparations.

Mellow joined her first, bringing the pitcher of iced tea with her. "This is going to be a long discussion, right?"

"If we can start the planning," Lena said. "Where are Scott and Tik?"

"On their way. I told them to grab the map and join us out here. It's nice to be able to sit outside again." Mellow dragged over the small table that sat at the other end of the porch. "Even for a little while."

Lena didn't want to fill the time with discussions about the weather, but she couldn't think of another topic. And sitting in silence was just too weird. "What did you tell them?"

"We wanted to see what they were planning," Mellow said. "Is it wrong that I want to surprise them?"

Lena grinned. The secrecy was making the whole thing fun. "Think of it as waiting until we have time to talk it through," she said. "When else would we have done it?"

Mellow pulled the last chair into place before saying, "This morning before we all got up? Last night before we went to sleep?"

"Fine, but I wasn't ready to do it then."

The door opened and Scott walked through with the map under one arm and a handful of papers in his right hand, and a glass of the vodka that came out of the new settlement at the fort abandoned by Newton Cole's men. "Ready to do what?"

Tik followed with three more glasses. "Thought we might want to test out the new batch."

Lena watched carefully as they laid the map out, using the glasses to hold down the corners. Scott placed his sheets of paper in front of him and pulled out a pencil. "Tik and I have figured out our plan. It'll be good to list the supplies, make sure we don't leave you short of anything."

"Before you do," Lena said, "Mellow and I have decided to come."

She expected an argument or a blank refusal to take them along. Scott looked at Tik and smiled. "You owe me a week's worth of kitchen duty."

She hadn't expected it. "Why didn't you ask us to come at the beginning?"

Tik smoothed the map before looking up. "We thought it would be more fun. And if it was your idea, then you'd be more committed."

"So, when Scott asked me to join you, he wasn't joking?"

Tik snapped his gaze back to Scott. "Cheat."

Scott laughed and slapped him on the back. "Yeah, yeah. They weren't getting on board fast enough. We need to leave next week, and I didn't want to go through our plans more than once. And we won't be here long enough for you to pay up anyway."

Lena picked up her vodka, trying to keep her smile under control. She really couldn't blame them for playing games. There wasn't all that much entertainment available at the farm, and she'd been doing pretty much the same.

"Show us the route," Mellow said. "We can't figure out supplies until we decide where we're going."

"We're traveling light," Scott said. "Plan is to stock up as we go. Do some hunting and fishing, maybe forage. I'm more concerned about having enough ammo."

"We should take the bows," Mellow said. "We can always make arrows, and it would take way more to pack guns, and the ammo would run out pretty quick."

Lena thought about the supplies they'd need to take to get them to their first stop. "We'll take the jerky and some dried apples. We'll pack some bread, but it won't last long."

"Maybe we can stop in Crystal, ask if they can supply us a bit," Tik said.

"No," Scott said before Lena could answer. "They will want to add someone. The more people in our party, the slower we go."

Lena didn't want to waste this night on trivial issues. An argument about stopping in a town they already knew was just that — trivial. "We can't leave the farm so short handed. Four of us gone means the planting might not be done in time. Keith will be in charge while we're gone. We need to ask him about bringing help in. Maybe Pallavi and Evan will come."

"And we should talk to Deb about what she can spare for medical supplies," Mellow said.

"And we need to tell everyone," Tik said. "And a thousand other tasks before we go."

"There are probably a thousand more things we aren't even thinking about. But it will all be sorted soon. When we leave, Keith can deal with the farm." Lena lifted her glass. "We should drink to our success."

_____

4

Lena packed her bedroll on Angel. Maya had appointed herself horse-namer at the farm, and Lena had no idea where the girl got her inspiration. Angel was their pack horse, but she was no different from the other horses. Lena's carried the interesting name of Bebop. Scott's rather plain looking mare had been dubbed Beauty. Mellow rode River, and Tik was on Storm.

The horses had their own corral at this camp, and most of the time they were hobbled to keep them close. The group decided early on that old rest areas were the best overnight camps as long as they checked the area carefully. So far, the plan had worked.

It had been a week since they passed through Crystal and picked up a list of items people wanted. No one had offered to join them, thank goodness.

Crystal wanted knowledge more than items. If anyone nearby was starting up a complementary craft. Books on building windmills and other potential energy sources. Solar panels were too delicate to transport on horseback, but a location would be an immense help. The thought of electricity powering the farm equipment, and maybe a communication channel, made Lena eager to search.

"We need to take some side trips," Scott said. "These roads are built to move people from one big place to another."

Most of the on- and off-ramps were intact. Many of those that were destroyed showed evidence that it happened recently, with purpose, cutting off a section of the land.

"Sounds good," Lena said. "We don't have any vulnerable people with us this time, so we should be able to handle problems if we stick together." The thought of having to fight off someone in their way didn't dim her excitement.

"And we're not scavenging," Mellow said. "No threat."

Tik looked around as if he expected to be surrounded by an army. He'd been jumpy for a few days. Lena wanted to talk to him about it, but she suspected he'd lie to her. "Just because we know we aren't a threat doesn't mean people will believe it."

"We won't know until we try," Lena said. "If we just ride straight through, we won't learn anything. That includes whether we seem like a threat to other communities."

"The next stable off-ramp?" Scott asked.

Tik mounted his horse, Storm, grabbed the reins of the pack animal and scanned the edge of the rest area again as everyone else prepared to leave. "As long as it's early enough in the day to move on if we don't find anything. And a couple of us scout the area first."

THREE HOURS later they found what they were looking for. An intact ramp with the highway sign still attached. Four communities used to exist within ten miles of the highway.

"We won't go too far," Scott said. "If the closest places are abandoned, we can pick a direction and follow the road for two or maybe three hours. That should give us time to return to the highway before we have to stop for the night."

"Keep your eyes out for a place to sleep as we go," Lena said. "Might give us more leeway to keep looking."

"Don't forget these side trips cost us distance," Tik said. "A day here and there might add up to us not making the coast in time."

"And running for the coast won't give us what we came out here to find," Mellow said in a tone that meant they'd had this discussion too many times.

THE RIDE from the freeway exit was very different. Whatever kept the major routes more or less clear and smooth was missing on the smaller roads. Potholes forced them onto the narrow shoulders to ride in a line, or heaves pushed them farther into the land on the side because of irrigation ditches.

"We might have to turn back soon," Lena said. "It's feeling a bit like we're being herded with all these barriers."

"And I haven't seen any sign of a town, let alone one that still has people." Tik stood on his stirrups as if it would give him an advantage. "We must have ridden the ten miles to the farthest town. We still have time to try another direction if we turn back." He'd been more settled when they left the highway despite his reservations.

Lena didn't want to give up on their first try at connecting with a new community, but there was nothing in sight. "The distance on the signs used to indicate the center of town. Maybe we missed a turn off, or it's just a farming community. I'm good with whatever you decide. I mean, we can camp on one of the larger shoulders if it gets too late."

Scott was looking around at the trees that had been planted as wind breaks.

"Anyone want to climb one of those maples? The land is fairly flat. I'd like to know if there's something we can't see before we turn back."

Lena didn't bother offering. Her tree climbing days were over, and it had never been fun for her.

"I'll do it," Tik said. He handed Storm's reins to Mellow and jumped the ditch to jog to the closest tree.

Lena watched as he scrambled up the branches until he was almost at the top. If he fell, there would be nothing they could do to stop him, and the drop would likely kill him. She saw him lean forward, peering off to the west. Mellow gasped in a breath.

"He'll be fine," Scott said. "I think he's happy to get a good look at the land. What's he so jumpy about, Mellow?"

So, it wasn't just me worrying unnecessarily, Lena thought.

"He won't tell me," Mellow said. "Remember when we first left the city? When he was scared of the gangs coming to take him back?"

"He got over that," Lena said.

"Maybe on the farm, but we're back on the road." Mellow sighed in relief as Tik leaped the ditch again.

"There's a water tower just a mile or two ahead. They had those in towns, right?"

"It's worth going on," Scott said. "If it turns out to be abandoned, we'll have a place to sleep."

Tik shrugged. "I guess it's a bit early to be worried about winter anyway."

5

Lena dismounted and walked toward the gates. The community they'd expected was locked up tight and this was the only entrance. There was no name on the rock that clearly had once held a large sign. The holes were still filled with the splinted remains of posts.

"It could mean anything," she said to the others. "If we can attract someone's attention, they might unlock the gate."

"I'm not climbing over that wall," Tik said. "I can see pointed stuff on the top. Spikes or broken glass would be my guess. I don't think they're getting ready to roll out the welcome mat."

Lena turned to face the others. "I think we can respect their desire for privacy. It doesn't mean they won't talk."

She inspected the gate for a way to call a resident to them. The gates were not part of the original design. The damage to the brickwork where someone had drilled bolts through to secure the ironwork was obvious. Also about ten feet inside was the mechanism for the barrier and an intact gatehouse.

"There has to be some way," she said. "They must rely

on hunting, and I don't see enough room inside for a decent field."

"Doesn't mean they want visitors." Scott joined her. "I've seen this kind of thing before. When I traveled solo. There'll be some kind of schedule for deliveries. Hunters and gatherers will go out when they know they won't be observed. Not everyone knows the plague is over. Not everyone believes the world isn't overrun by some kind of mutants."

The whole day was a waste. Tik was right. All she'd done was delay their progress. If too many communities were like this, locked and forbidding, she'd never take her vision from a dream to a reality.

Mellow stepped up beside her. "They must have a way to summon a guard. Surely unexpected visitors aren't all unwelcome."

She leaned against the side of the gate and peered in. The bars were too close for her to do anything but slip an arm inside. "Here." Mellow strained to reach for something and drew out a thick rope. "It's attached to a bell." She yanked it a couple of times.

Lena hear a distant clang. "We can wait an hour, right? And still get back to the road?"

Tik, who was holding all the reins, shook his head. "It will be dark before we make it all the way back. We'll camp on a clearing early enough to scout out any dangers and get going at dawn."

Maybe they would take the time to search in a different direction before they headed up the on-ramp. One of the other communities the sign named might be welcoming. She kept the thought to herself. She'd pushed Tik's original objection as far as she could today. No point in stoking the fire and spoiling the ride back with an argument.

"Let's mount up," Scott said. "I don't want anyone

spooking the horses while we're down here. Tik can't hold all of them if they decide to bolt."

IT DIDN'T TAKE LONG for a woman to come to the gate. She was dressed in loose clothes of undyed homespun cloth. Her hair pulled into a braid and wrapped around her head. A hatchet hung from her right hand. "We don't let strangers in."

Lena slipped to the ground again and hurried to the gate. She couldn't let the woman walk away without telling them something.

"Could we talk to the community leader?" she asked.

"You think I can't be that? You think I'd send out someone I swore to protect? I don't know what kind of trouble you bring."

"Lots of leaders would stay in safety. My name is Lena."

"I go by Mother. You be as friendly as you want, still not getting in."

Lena conceded the point. "Just a little information would be great."

"You got five minutes."

No one was wearing a watch to keep her to the time limit. Lena figured the five minutes would last as long as Mother was interested. A horse behind her whickered and shifted weight. "Can you tell us about the area? We're just passing through, no plans to settle."

Mother looked over their group. Her expression remained stubborn. "Why are you on the road? It's not safe."

It was a good question but suddenly saying "just checking out the world" felt like a stupid answer. Lena didn't want to stumble through an explanation for this woman who was clear she wouldn't help. "I think it's more dangerous to not worry about what's going on around us. We left home weeks ago to scout for any dangers. Do you have any details?"

Mother stared at Lena without speaking for a while — or that's what it felt like. After what felt like forever, she nodded as if she'd won an argument with herself. "Yeah. I hear you. We aren't looking to expand. Hard enough to support the people who live here now. We scout too, but not so far. There's a couple of towns south of the highway. Don't seem like a threat, but who knows? We all just keep our distance so as not to bring trouble."

"No one leaves here?" Lena couldn't imagine a place where everyone was willing to just stick around. She suspected a story beneath Mother's statement that she didn't want to tell.

"Markets, we head out to one every month. I make people go find a mate from outside. Someone willing to come in and follow our rules so we don't breed ourselves into raving idiots. Other than that and new babies, we stay about the same size population. No one leaves permanent."

"We're heading east from here," Lena said. "Any tips?"

"Get on the old highway and keep going. You won't make it by tonight. You remember passing a closed ARCO station?"

It was about halfway back to their road. "Yes."

"We set it up as a safe place to camp. Not the Ritz, but it's clean. Leave it that way when you head out."

"Thanks, we were a bit worried about tonight. The markets? Where are they held?"

Mother tapped her wrist like she was wearing a watch. She nodded to the three on horses behind Lena, turned and walked away.

6

"It's too peaceful," Tik said. "We should be hearing birds at least. And some wild dogs? They were baying last night."

"The dogs are sleeping now," Mellow said. "The wild ones are more active when their prey is vulnerable."

Tik's anxiety was infecting Lena and maybe the others in the group. No one else spoke up, so Lena kept her thoughts to herself. Perhaps the sense of being observed was just a reaction to the peaceful ride. Or something about her expectations of danger and the reality of the road.

AN HOUR LATER, Scott urged his horse to walk beside Lena's. "We're being followed," he said. "Through the fields. At least two riders."

"Yes, both on the north side, right?"

"Like we're being escorted past someone's territory. I think we should speed up, see if that puts them off."

South was just open fields with a hint of greenhouses in the distance. Nowhere to hide any observers. Lena glanced at the windbreak of trees that followed the road on the other side. Whatever was farmed needed protecting from the elements, and observers. There were no laws now, so it wasn't to protect someone from identifying an illegal crop. It would be about value, or the power it gave to control others. "I can only think of two crops, neither of them grow here. Marijuana needs shade and moisture, opium needs far more sun and dry soil."

"Food might be a better option," Scott said.

"What does Tik think?" Lena asked.

"We can't see past the trees, so it could be anything under a plastic or glass roof. Plastic sheeting is still available to scavenge."

"I think we should stop when we get a chance on the safe side of the road. Talk about it as a group." She glanced back down the line of horses. "Running might make our escorts suspicious. It would be normal to make a stop soon."

"Pretend we haven't realized anyone is tracking us?" Scott glanced to the side again. "Might be too late."

They had no safe option, Lena thought. "I can't ride the day out with all this anxiety. We don't know how far they'll keep tabs on us. Or what they will interpret as a threat."

IT WAS early afternoon by the time they found a place to stop that was big enough for all of them and the horses to rest. Tik handed out bread and cheese, Mellow tended to the horses and Lena watched for action across the street as she filled a bucket from the irrigation ditch to water their rides. Since farmers had abandoned their fields, or the use of pesticides, the ditch was clean if you were fine with the stale taste of the water.

"You don't provoke them," Tik said as they stood eating.

"I say we keep moving at the same pace. They are happy to just observe right now, and anything can change that."

"Like us camping for the night?" Lena asked. "I don't want them deciding to kill us in our sleep. It's better if we have some control. Not like provoking an attack, but at least contact?"

"There's no difference," Tik said. "I don't think they are following us to find a good place to chat. They'll attack and leave us dead as a warning."

Tik's reaction to any hint of gang activity was always over the top. Lena understood his reaction; he'd been targeted by his own gang before they fled New Surrey. But she couldn't let fear put the group at risk.

"Too late," Mellow said. "They are coming."

Tik took a handful of arrows from the quiver on his back. They would stab as well as fly.

Three men crossed the road on horseback. All wore black clothes that looked like they were well cared for. Two of the men had wounds on their cheeks that would heal into the brand on the third's face. A circle with a lightning bolt across it.

"Move on," the man with the scar said. "Out of our territory by dark or you'll be dead."

"How far is your territory?" Tik asked. "We don't know you, so help us out."

"What are you doing on our road?"

"Traveling through," Lena said. "There were no signs, so how were we to know you held this area?"

"I don't answer questions," the man said. "You keep moving and you'll pass out of our territory before dark. You stop again and we'll take that as a reason to kill you and go home to a hot meal and a soft bed."

Tik stepped between Lena and the man. "You attack, and

we'll fight. Why did you bother to talk to us? We were moving through, not even coming close to your fields, or whatever is behind the trees. So, we'll keep going if you leave us alone."

That was a good point, Lena thought. Why make it obvious?

The man leaned down close to Tik's face. "We don't take chances. You keep moving. We keep watching. One wrong move and we end you."

Tik's back tightened and he raised the hand gripping the arrows.

"Stop," Lena said. "We'll move on. We have no interest in whatever you are doing. But like he said, we won't go down easy if you try to attack."

The man looked at her, and then turned his horse back to the road. The two other men followed and disappeared through the windbreak.

7

"We should have run into other travelers," Tik said. His jumpiness had returned each time they came back to the highway.

Mellow added a branch to their fire and brushed the dirt from her hands before speaking. "You think there's trouble ahead of us?"

"Don't you? Or can you think of a reason no one is moving along the road?" Tik pulled his pack toward the fire and removed his copy of the map. "We're coming close to the exits for some decent sized towns. Not really exits. The highway skirts the edges. I think we should at least take some back ways around."

"You think gangs took all the cities?" Lena asked. "I'm happy to step off the highway and explore the outlying communities, but you wanted to move faster."

Scott helped Tik anchor the map on the ground close enough to the fire for light, but away from the range of the sparks. Mellow shifted to Tik's side and leaned in to help find a path.

"Tik has a point," Scott said. "I imagine these bigger communities don't have resources. They were built on the expectation that food and other supplies would come in and their waste would go out, right?"

Lena was the only one in the group old enough to have firsthand knowledge of living in the world before. "Not quite that specific. What really happened is they grew into that. And the work was sometimes specialized. A few gardens in backyards, if the city hadn't used all the land for apartments. But what we did, and eventually the rest of the small towns that followed Poorjohn, is probably the same as others. Unless you had a way to sustain yourself, the city was a bad place to stay."

Tik traced a wandering line to the north of the highway. "I know we want to trend south, but the shorter diversion is north. We'll be adding a couple more days to our journey than if we ride straight through, but it's better to avoid attracting the wrong attention, right?"

Lena joined the rest of the group kneeling at the map. "What if we went south? Could we link up with the highway farther along?"

"It kind of zigzags until what was North Dakota," Mellow said. "We could join and exit a few times before we have to find a highway that goes more west than south."

Lena scanned the entire map. It wasn't detailed enough to show even mid-sized towns, let alone small ones. She missed the ability to zoom in and out on a phone to see the detail level she needed. Of course, even with GPS, it was always possible that sparsely populated areas wouldn't have service.

The conversation around her had continued while she thought, and now they were looking to find faster, or at least different routes. Their only focus seemed to be getting as far as Seattle before winter.

She felt her purpose slipping away as the discussion continued. "We need a reason," she said. "If we know why we're traveling, we can set a route. One that allows us to be flexible depending on what we find."

"Okay," Tik said. "I get it. My reason is for us to scope out any potential trouble without bringing it back to the farm."

"The fastest route might not do that," Mellow said. "I'm with Tik more or less. I want to see what's out here, maybe come home with some new ideas."

"Me too, at first," Scott said. "Planning this out back at the farm was okay, but now that we've seen some of the places people made into homes, I'm not sure it's as simple as checking things out. I guess I didn't really have a purpose other than itchy feet."

Lena sat back on her heels and thought for a moment. Scott's words resonated. She came with a vague idea of a future created out of unity with other towns and villages. But there had been no commonality with any of the places they'd visited so far. She was trying to build the final vision before she had enough information.

"I did have an idea of why I came," she said. "Yes, I was getting a bit restless, and I didn't want to be separated from you, Scott, for so long. But I don't want to just scope out what's happening. I want to start bringing people together."

"Hard over long distances," Tik said. "No communications means fracturing, right?"

"I have to believe that if we pool our ideas and resources, we can solve a lot of the problems. Maybe not bring back what we had, but start the process of getting close."

"How do you mean?" Scott asked. "You think someone is finding a way to produce enough power to get a communication system up and running? Or a way to fuel a vehicle so we don't rely on horses?"

"I do, I guess. Of course, some people will try to use whatever they develop to exert power, but not everyone. And wouldn't a tractor be more useful at the farm than a horse attached to a plow?"

8

"You're quiet," Mellow's voice cut through Lena's thoughts. "Anything wrong?"

They were riding along a tree-lined road. The area must have been buffer land. A strip of empty field between farm and residential or light industry. They hadn't seen a cross street for hours. The sky was clear and the sun uncomfortable enough to force the horses to the slight shade on the north side.

"Just thinking," Lena said, "about last night."

"Have you changed your mind?" Mellow nudged her horse closer as if trying to stop the men hearing their conversation.

"Not about the route. I'm thinking about what I want for the future."

The discussion last night ended with an agreement to wend their way southwest and stay off the highway unless they needed to cross a river. It meant the occasional backtrack, when the bridge labeled on the map turned out to have collapsed.

So far, they hadn't come across any small towns, or even

a sign to one. Still, half a day was too early to decide whether the plan was good or a mistake. The need for patience was easy to grasp, hard to implement.

"I came along because I didn't want to be apart from Scott, or I didn't want to have to wonder what happened." Lena tried to grab hold of the feeling. Last night's discussion had opened a view on her goal that she still needed to process.

Mellow giggled. "Yeah. Scott and Tik need someone to keep them safe."

"True." Lena glanced ahead at the two men. They were chatting about something. The buzz of insects and heaviness of the heat kept their voices muted. "But I really wanted to see if we could reunite again. Not as a country or two countries. But something that will bring back some of the things we used to have. Closer back to normal, I guess."

"So far, we haven't found anyone even ready to talk," Mellow said.

"It's a long trip. I'm not getting discouraged. I don't know how to talk about it, I guess. It's been a while since I've had to sell anyone on an idea."

THEY STOPPED to rest the horses and fill their water bottles at an abandoned gas station. This was the first crossroad they'd come across. No signs to help decide what direction they should take. Inside the building, the contents of the shelves were gone, and had been for a long time.

A stand with postcards and maps of the area lay on its side. Scott and Tik picked over the detailed charts like kids with a new Lego set. "Local stuff." Scott showed her a brochure with a map to some attractions. "We should look for more of these as we go. We can burn the paper or leave the ones we don't need for someone else when we leave the area."

"Is there a community close to us?" Lena craned her neck to read the directions. "I'm getting tired of open land and trees."

"Tik and I will check them all out," Scott said. "We'll only take the ones that look like they'll help. Unless you think the corn maze is still running."

Lena laughed, her languor lifting now that they were in a cooler environment. "I'll have a look in the back. Maybe find something we can use."

The back of the station was not exactly stocked. The scavenging had been less destructive, and by the look of the cartons on the floor, whoever ransacked was looking for beer. She found a box of jerky under a pile of empty cans.

"Need some help?"

Mellow's question startled Lena. "I almost had a heart attack."

"Sorry," Mellow said as she stepped closer to where Lena was digging into the debris.

"No problem. I shouldn't have let my guard down." She pointed to the far corner. "Be careful as you go through it. There are a few smashed bottles."

Mellow gently lifted sheets of cardboard, setting some aside. "I was thinking about what you said."

"Yeah?"

"Do you really think everyone wants to get back to normal?"

"Why not? I mean, we'd be more careful with agreements to make sure they were fair all around, but this living hand to mouth isn't sustainable. Birth control isn't available anymore. Soon we'll have too many people to support the way we do it now."

Mellow dragged a box from the corner. "Magazines. I know we can't take them all, but some?"

"As many as we can carry," Lena said. "We'll discard them as we read or offer them in exchange for food. The load won't be heavy for long."

Mellow went to the horses and grabbed a sack. While she was gone, Lena scanned the magazines. Celebrity gossip — most of them would be long dead. A technology issue about artificial intelligence — the singularity had not happened. Two different issues of Popular Mechanics and a handful of crafting and cooking magazines.

Mellow stuffed the sack with as many as it would take. "Not everyone had a good life before. Some people lived hand to mouth or by begging."

It took Lena a second to realize Mellow was continuing their conversation.

"We're less polarized now," she said. "There's hope we can make the future better."

"I didn't mean that, but don't assume people aren't taking strong sides," Mellow said. "You don't know how people are interpreting what you say. Back to normal for you is a kinder life with some luxuries, right?"

"It's not quite that simple." Lena kept her tone neutral; she didn't want Mellow to realize she was annoyed.

"My back to normal means working at a menial job until I get married, and maybe after that, too. I know I was a kid before, but my parents were poor. Your life was easier than most, even after."

Her voice held no anger or blame. A simple statement of facts.

"Okay. Are you saying I need to take that into account? Like I'm assuming too much?"

"I'm saying you need to accept that some people prefer

life the way it is, so be very clear about what you mean by normal."

"I will. I guess Tik and Scott might have different ideas too."

"Talking to them might be a good way to start. Find out what they think needs to change. Even if people agree, you can't be sure if they mean it as you do or see it as a way to grab power and control people. I can't fit any more in here; are you ready to head out?"

9

They'd spent a week checking out the small communities on the maps. Most were simply abandoned, tiny towns, barely a crossroads with a tavern, store, and gas station. It must be difficult to sustain a decent life with only a few people left to help. Lena assumed the residents had all moved along to join other places where they could contribute and thrive.

In one of those tiny gas station towns, they explored houses and found evidence that no one had survived. Two skeletons laid peacefully on a bed. Not a common sight this long after the plague burned itself out, but the residence had been locked up, so no larger scavenging animals to take the body apart for food.

Now, they sat on their horses at the end of a long street that led to yet another gated community. This one hadn't started that way. It was clear that early on someone had designed the walls and gates like something out of a post-apocalyptic movie. Panels of corrugated metal with rust patches and overly large cross bars.

"They know we're here," Tik said. "If you want to talk to

someone inside, we should knock now before they get suspicious."

"I know it's stupid," Lena said, "but I can't get over the idea that whoever built the barricade is dangerous."

"Or they have powerful enemies," Tik said.

"If they wanted to attack, they've had plenty of opportunity," Scott said.

Lena fought against her instinct to run and nudged Bebop forward. Inhabited towns were too hard to find to avoid any.

"Stay where you are," a voice called from a guard tower.

"We're not here to cause trouble," Lena called back. "Just us four. Passing through."

"Said, stay there. Someone will come to talk."

The sound of boots on metal stairs followed.

"I guess we wait," Tik said. "I don't like it. I should ride around a bit to make sure they aren't trying to flank us."

"Stay," Lena said. "I don't want them thinking we're scouting the place for weakness. If they don't come soon, we can just leave."

It felt like defeat to even consider riding away, but Lena couldn't take the chance they'd be stuck somewhere unpleasant for the night. Especially if the residents here were what the walls communicated. Paranoid and ready for a fight.

"Sorry to keep you waiting."

The voice came from the left side of the metal gate. Lena turned to find a middle aged man dressed in overalls smiling up at her, a small door standing open behind him.

"How can we help you?"

"We were hoping for a night's rest and some conversation," Lena said.

"Strangers are welcome at Beta as long as they don't cause trouble and agree to leave if we say so."

It wasn't hostile, and not completely welcoming either. "My name is Lena. We don't have any reason to cause trouble."

"Name's Michael." The man nodded to the others. "Introductions can wait until we've settled the horses and given you a chance to clean up. Ride around the left and you'll find our stables. George will show you where to go."

George showed them to a stall for all of their horses. "Used to be a big riding stable before. Take care of the animals and I'll show you around while someone gets your rooms ready."

"Why all the protection?" Tik asked as he rubbed down Storm. "You don't seem to mind visitors."

"Had some problems early on. People wanted what we made and thought it was a good idea to take it. Just got used to it, I guess."

"What do you make?" Scott asked as he filled the water trough.

"You finish up here and I'll show you," George said. "There'll be hot water in the rooms for you to clean up later. We eat in a couple of hours."

Lena brushed the last of the sweat from Bebop, thinking of how great a bath would be, even if it was cold. And time to wash clothes. "I'd like to talk to the person in charge. Is that possible?"

"Da Vinci isn't here right now, be back in a couple of days. Give you time to see what living here is like. You got skills we can use, you might get invited to stay."

Mellow sorted through their packs. "Can we leave stuff here?"

"It'll be safe, and you can come back anytime to check or pick up something you need. Ready?"

They followed George through the barn to the entrance to the town. It must have been a college or something before. The buildings they passed were built of brick and creamy stone, the grounds turned to vegetable gardens retained the look of a quad.

"We call this place Beta," George said. "Seemed reasonable given the work we do. Come on in here."

'Here' was a low building that differed from the others. Made of concrete and glass, the interior was flooded with natural light at this time of day, but Lena saw lanterns around the walls, and on tables. Men and women worked at what looked like engines on the table, and in the far corner, ten bicycles were wired up to car batteries.

"You have power?" she asked, shocked.

"Yup. Not a lot, and we work hard to keep the batteries topped up. This is what we do. Try to find a way to bring back stuff we miss. Nothing big, mind you. Not a computer, takes too much power and none of us are coders. But we might be able to fix it so people can have light, or cars. Powered with clean energy. Takes more work than a gas engine, but we don't got any way to refine fuel around here. And it's not like there's a lot taking our time."

Mellow dug around in her pack. "We found these," she said, handing George the magazines they'd found in the gas station.

George looked them over and handed back the one featuring artificial intelligence. "I'll pass them on to the archivist. These craft ones will come in handy if we decide we can work on stuff like automating looms, and our cooks could use a few new recipes. I'll give them back when you go."

George led them to a tall dorm building and handed them the keys to two suites. "Showers down the hall. We have hot water, but not a lot, so be warned: it could run out."

10

Lena sat in the fabrication observation room with big headphones covering her ears. They protected her from noise but made it impossible to have a conversation. She was with Michael, the man who'd greeted them only two days ago. In the time they'd spent waiting for the leader to return, the residents took advantage of the opportunity to talk to new people about their progress.

Scott was off looking at the plans for farm equipment improvements, Mellow in a small pharmacy where the scientists were attempting to reproduce some basic medicines. Tik was talking to an armorer about a faster arrow production process.

In this space, Lena was restricted to a chair in a room looking through a large window at the activity. The noise was coming from only a few machines, grinding and banging metal into shapes. Micheal had explained the need to husband the electricity to power only the most efficient equipment. Where human power could be used, it was.

Human power ranged from using tools to complete the fine work after the brute force machine had finished the general shaping, to pulling on belts or working a treadle as large as a seesaw instead of plugging into a battery. Everyone on the floor was wearing protective gear, but they seemed able to communicate even over the noise.

Michael tapped her shoulder and pointed to the door leading outside. He motioned for her to keep the ear protectors on until they were outside. He drew her along a path through what must have been the agricultural sciences. A meandering walk by fields just turning green as the plants raised their heads, and a grove of trees.

In the grounds, Lena sighed at the peace. "I'm guessing it's not quite as noisy as that kind of factory would have been before?"

"Not noticeably, but it's just a foundry. We don't have what it takes to work a factory, nor do we have the demand to spend time trying to make it work," Michael said. "About the only thing I remember from before that we don't get now is that background buzz from the electric power. It was the thing you kind of carried home after work. Like tinnitus. Most of us working in there take this path after shift. Gives us a quiet time to enjoy a little peace."

"How will you scale up?" Lena asked, pulling her hair into a ponytail to relieve some of the heat. "You are planning to, right?"

"Long term, yeah." Michael steered her toward the food hall. "There's a lot to think about before we go too far. Only so much material, and power. We're looking into stuff from the past. Generating power from a river run, solar, wind. Anything we can do easy and will work pretty much anywhere."

"Is there anything we can do to help while we travel?" Lena wanted Michael to accept her as an ally by the time their leader returned. Places like Beta were important to her vision.

Michael poured them both a glass of iced tea and led her to a table in the corner. "Da Vinci does most of the thinking on the future. We like to build things and make things work."

"It looks like you're pretty successful at it," she said.

"Most of us need to do this stuff, like a calling. Da Vinci is good at focusing us. Otherwise, we'd be all over the place with new projects and discarded ones. Like kids, right?"

Lena could imagine what Michael meant. Following passion didn't always result in useful work. It was the same at the farm; plenty of routine jobs that would be neglected if she didn't manage people.

"Did those magazines help?"

Michael gulped his tea. "Maybe. The archivist will go through them and see. Problem with most publications from before is they rely on technology we don't have. So, they talk about using design apps when we have to draw a schematic on graph paper."

Lena chuckled. "I sometimes envy the younger generation. They don't know how easy things were. It's like I have to translate ideas from one language to another. What we did before to how we can do this now."

"And should we do it now," Michael said. "Lots of things made the world worse. That's one of the things Da Vinci is thinking about. How we avoid making things that can be used to take power."

"If someone wants to use something as a weapon, they'll find a way," Lena said. "A rock can kill someone."

"Yeah, but no one really needed an atomic bomb, no matter how many inventions came from it."

"Good point," Lena said. "I wish Da Vinci luck on that score."

"There's also more mundane questions. Like how we transport stuff. How we tell people about it. We've got a team working on some kind of telegraph system using the remaining infrastructure, at least the stuff that hasn't broken over the years."

"Communication across the country would be useful," Lena said. She didn't want to dive into the details of her vision until she was talking to Da Vinci, but communication was one of her main needs to gain some unity.

"No, the world." Michael waved his arm as if encompassing the entire globe. "Those undersea cables are still in place, and they were built last."

"Are other countries working on it too?" Lena had assumed the continent was cut off.

"No idea. But ships are, lots of the old sailing ships are seaworthy with a bit of repairs. Soon people will be out looking for trade, or just information."

"Or colonizing?" Lena asked.

"Yeah, there's always assholes who think they can own what they want. I figure most people now can recognize the early signs. Make it harder to do."

Lena hoped he was right.

"Your friends are here," Michael said with a nod to the door. "I'll let you catch up. Da Vinci is expected back tomorrow. If I don't have a chance to say it later, good luck on your journey. Stop on your way back and tell us about what you found."

His words chilled Lena. She'd gotten comfortable in the couple of days they'd been in Beta. Michael made it sound like they might be turfed out without notice if this Da Vinci guy didn't care for them.

11

Dinner was a more formal affair than the other meals they'd taken over the last few days in Beta. Da Vinci, the leader, had returned that morning and declared they would celebrate and talk over a meal. His scavenging trip had been successful, a wagon load of metal and four deer.

Da Vinci was in his fifties, lean and tall with a slight stoop, which probably came from leaning over a keyboard or worktable for most of his life. He seemed friendly and welcoming, but Lena remembered Micheal's words. Da Vinci was as likely to send them on their way as he was to offer them shelter.

"I know I should leave it to others, this ranging out and collecting material, but I like seeing what's going on and how far we have to range." He passed a bowl of potato salad to Lena. "It won't be long before the old body stops me, so I take advantage."

"You trade locally?" Lena asked. Talking about his local reach might raise the subject of wider unity. And if he had agreements, it would help her understand the possibilities better.

"I don't know if you'd call it trade," he said. "I'm told you've been touring around Beta. Did anyone give you our history?"

Lena glanced around the table to see if the others had an answer. Micheal, George, and a woman named Diz had joined them. Lena wasn't sure if it was as a reward for acting as tour guides, or to verify what any of them said.

"You're mostly made up of teachers and students from the university," Scott said. "That's all I've heard. We were far too interested in the present than the past. Your setup is impressive."

"At the start," Michael said. "People would come and go. The first couple of years were tricky. But after that, we got a bit of a rep for what we do. Locals around steer people to us if they seem likely."

"And you'll have noticed it's not just scholars and engineers. We're a real little town with all kinds of services," Da Vinci said.

Lena thought back to the last few years at the farm. None of Cole's men stuck around, but a few of the people in Poorjohn's congregation asked to stay. "How do you know who to keep?"

George grunted at her question. "We've made a few mistakes. And not all mistakes were ours. A few people tried to stick with us, but they couldn't. Too big an itch to wander. And a few people lied about their abilities."

"We do try to align people with their skills," Da Vinci said. "As I said, we're a real town. But we learned pretty quickly to set some tests. People have to prove they can do what they claim and do it under real conditions. Like a machinist who can't adapt to the fact we have no power machines isn't going to fit. Not in that job anyway. And we encourage people to let the past go. To change their names if they like. I wasn't always Da Vinci, but his imagination and drive always inspired me."

"Anyone try to stay who you wanted to go?" Tik asked. "We had some trouble like that back home."

"A few, but what can you do?" Diz said. "We aren't violent, and we don't have jails. We make it uncomfortable for them, I guess. Menial jobs. A bit of light shunning. They either change or go eventually."

"Trouble with gangs?" Tik asked.

"None, lately. We try to keep note of gang territory as we range out for materials, but they are hard to pin down. The gangs expand and contract like living organisms," Da Vinci said. "Like I said, I don't believe in violence, but we have a lot of sharp, pointy things like arrows. And good walls. Any gang that tries to take us over tends to believe our threats."

"I saw your armory," Tik said. "Good arrows."

"We make tools to survive," George said. "So, arrows and knives, crossbows, bolts. No swords, and no guns — they are a little complicated anyway. I know people can use what we do make for bad intentions, but it's less easy than if we put swords in people's hands."

"Let's hope you can keep it that way," Lena said. "We're on the road for a while, checking out how people have survived. I'm hoping to help pull a kind of country out of all the different communities."

"An ambitious dream," Da Vinci said. "You'll remember how chaotic the country was before. Everyone had their own idea of right and were unwilling to listen to alternatives. I like the value approach. We trade for things we need, not for power."

Lena sighed. "I'm hoping people have moved past that

phase. Not having their own ideas of right, there's nothing wrong with that, but self righteousness? It doesn't make for a good debate. We won't know how it might work until we've talked to a lot more people."

"You'll need a solid communications system," Da Vinci said. "We are making some headway on telegraphs. And travel. Could you observe and note any train lines you pass?"

"Aren't most of the trains useless now?" Scott asked. "I don't remember hearing about any solar powered engines."

"Leave that to us," Da Vinci said. "I am interested in the state of the tracks. We can always find a way to travel along them. And repair them. If we could refit wagons with wheels that fit over the tracks, strong ones that don't need constant maintenance, we could speed up travel across the country."

"We'll do our best," Lena said. "I'm not sure if we'll come this way back, but I'll figure out a way to get our findings to you. It won't be soon. Maybe a year."

"I wonder if we should put together an exploration ourselves," Da Vinci said. "Not as expansive as yours, of course. But focused on the possibilities. Even assessing the market for better plows, or training others to improve their methods."

"And my vision," Lena said. "If we have some success, would you sign on to an agreement to work together, a set of common rules?"

"I have no objection at this moment," Da Vinci said. "When you have tried with more communities, you must tell me more detail about what you expect. I'm not fully convinced that a concord between far flung communities is enforceable, even if you gain agreement."

"That's a problem for another day," Lena said.

12

"This was good for the horses," Mellow said the next morning.

They were preparing to leave Beta with what Lena hoped was a good start on building her vision. "And us, I think," she said. "We got some direction, and Da Vinci seems a bit interested in joining up communities."

Scott stacked the packs to be loaded on Angel, their pack horse. "I think he's more interested in gadgets. And he can build bigger and better ones if the communities come together."

True, but Lena wanted to think it was more than self-interest. "Those things go hand in hand. Unity needs communication and travel, he gets to lead those projects. If I can't get enough people to agree in principle, he has no reason to follow through with any of his grand ideas."

Tik hung one of the quivers of bolts Da Vinci had given them in exchange for information. The short crossbow was hanging on its strap around his shoulder, the other three were attached to the three saddles. "They do pretty well with just local stuff," he said. "These bows are easier to use and carry than ours."

The long bows they brought from the farm were unstrung and packed for Angel. The extra arrows for those were carefully rolled in their clothing to avoid bending the shafts.

"It's hard to look at them as just for hunting, though," Lena said. "Long bows are less effective in a fight, but these, more like handguns than hunting weapons."

Scott attached the final pack to Angel and tested the balance. "Yeah, but these are good for both. We have no idea what's out there. I'm happier being prepared."

Lena agreed with him. The road had been peaceful so far, but that was bound to change. And the longer it took before the next challenge, the more she expected worse than just being warned off. And the jumpier Tik got.

"This is the maximum load," Mellow said as she checked Angel's gait before taking the lead rein. "We'll need another pack horse if we keep amassing stuff."

"If we find a place to barter, we'll need to trade something." Scott checked the area to make sure all their belongings were loaded. "The only thing we have right now is the new weapons."

"I'd be happy to find a place with a market and figure out what to trade when we arrive," Lena said. "Michael said there are some around, but not close."

"I'm not sure we should trust everything we heard," Tik said. "Why would anyone be so honest with strangers?"

"Because Da Vinci wants the opportunity to supply his re-inventions to a huge market," Mellow said. "But you are right. We might be reading too much into this. It's the first place we've been welcomed, and that might be blinding us."

Lena checked Bebop's saddle for the third time. They

were alone in the stables — as far as she could tell. If anyone was listening, Da Vinci would know soon enough that he wasn't fully trusted. The conversation wasn't finished as far as she was concerned, but it would be better to continue it when they were on their way.

"Okay, you all have a point. I still want to take this as a win. No one here has given me any reason to doubt them. But we've only stayed a few days. And they were all in tour guide mode."

"Just a second," Tik said. He slipped out of the barn and returned a few minutes later. "No one is hanging around."

"Or they've already run to tell Da Vinci everything we said," Scott said. "We need to leave here and get on the road. I've gone from thinking this was a good rest to wondering if we're about to be waylaid, robbed, and killed."

"Yeah, but once we're gone, we can't check on any of our suspicions," Tik said. "I think we should go on a last walk around the grounds. See what happens when we surprise them."

"I'll stay with the horses," Mellow said. "I wouldn't know if I saw something wrong."

Lena hated that she'd been influenced, but she couldn't think of a reason to miss the opportunity to do a quick check. It wouldn't settle anyone's nerves, but it would give them something concrete to argue about. "I'll stay with Mellow. Most of my time was spent in places that you can't wander into. And come to think of it, I was never left alone to talk to anyone but Michael." Now she was worried. Had he lulled her into complacency?

Scott whispered something to Tik and then led him out.

"I don't like this," Mellow said. "I mean, sure we shouldn't just trust people, but this feels like a betrayal."

"You're right. And if they are exactly what we thought,

then we could be damaging a relationship. One that could help us no matter what happens with my plans."

"The boys will be careful," Mellow said. "And your vision is good. It's not what you want to make of the future, so much as... I don't know. Maybe you are moving too fast?"

"Like trusting anyone who kind of agrees with me?" Lena smiled to soften the words. When the idea first came to her, she was so certain. But now, learning that she was naive about how people might react, and suddenly questioning how trustworthy anyone was, she could see the plans slipping away the tighter she tried to control it.

"That's just happening because you are going too fast," Mellow said. "You had a pretty good idea of the future. Then you jumped right into trying to make it happen. Newton Cole and Poorjohn both had ideas of how the world should be."

"I'm not like that," Lena said. "I want people to partner with each other, not live under my rule."

"I know. But they don't."

Lena took a deep breath at Mellow's words. Before when she worked for people, she hated when they bulldozed a new idea into the job. And here she was pretty much doing the same thing.

Tik slipped back inside. "Let's go. Scott is on his way."

13

"There's a subdivision only a few hours' ride to the north," Lena said. She checked the list Da Vinci gave her along with general directions to the locations of his clients. Notes on anything he thought might be important were almost as valuable as the locations. This community had a line describing it as pretty conservative, but good customers for farming equipment. "If we push, we can make it before dusk. Camp nearby."

"I thought we decided to take his recommendations with a grain of salt," Scott said.

The discussion they started in the stable continued that night in camp. Nothing concrete came up, but Lena couldn't deny that each of them had a different kind of uneasy feeling about Beta.

"We did, and when we get to this place, I plan to be cautious. If we totally ignore his suggestions, we're going to end up on the west coast without talking to anyone. That's if we make it at all."

"I'm enjoying the ride," Mellow said. "I'm up for heading toward this place, but do we have to rush?"

Lena bit back her reaction. It had only been two days since they left Beta. She worried that they would travel past all the places Da Vinci listed and be stuck guessing again. Did it matter if they camped on the road? Arrive in this Sunny Meadows place in the morning?

"I thought we'd prefer the chance of a bed to camping again," she said. "We can just head in that direction. I'm hoping we can come away with directions to more towns. Trying to figure out where we go with just the maps isn't very efficient. We have no idea whether a community survived, let alone if it's a place to visit or avoid. We can't make it through this trip without taking a few chances."

"Yeah," Tik said. "And the places were pretty few and far between anyway. Not like up the east coast where every few miles you could find a quaint village."

He was way too young before the plague changed everything to remember how life used to be.

"I know what you're thinking, Lena. My parents took me on a road trip when I was just a kid."

"Am I that easy to read?"

Mellow laughed. "Every time anyone says anything about before, you get a look on your face. Like you're thinking about giving us a history lecture."

"Thanks. That doesn't make me feel old at all."

THEY CAMPED for the night early. Close enough to Sunny Meadows to reach it not long after daybreak, but far enough away to avoid causing alarm.

A megastore parking lot this time. The building was long emptied of anything useful, and it smelled of rats and unpleasant fluids. They set up at the edge where the horses could be safe and eat the grass and weeds that had grown up. A circle of RVs filled the center of the asphalt, all abandoned and stripped of anything that could be taken out.

"It would have been nice to find something to soften the ground," Mellow said. "I guess a sleeping bag is better than moldy cardboard or mattresses. Good thing it's warm enough we don't have to set a fire."

There would be worse places ahead of them, Lena thought. "We should find a way to light one anyway. I think we need to keep an eye out all night."

The horses whickered and stamped, then quieted down. Lena heard hoofs crossing the asphalt beyond the RV corral.

Scott and Tik were standing when she looked back. Their new crossbows pointed down and ready to raise and fire.

"Hello?" The words preceded the appearance of a single man walking a horse. The man was wearing jeans and a faded concert tee shirt, the lettering so worn that Lena couldn't guess at the name of the artist. He walked stooped forward like he was peering at the world before he chanced joining it. "Any chance you'd let a stranger join you? For the night?"

They had no claim on the camp and Lena didn't think letting him set up just out of sight was a smart choice. "We just got here. You are welcome to join us."

Scott shifted their sleeping bags to make room. Lena noticed that he placed the man between him and Tik. Good. Someone needed to keep an eye on him.

"Name's Luis," he said. "I'll just introduce Junior to your beasts."

"We keep a watch on the horses, all night," Scott said. "Being out here makes us careful, we switch off so no one gets too tired."

The man nodded and wandered toward the animals.

"He might be useful if he's traveled around here." Lena kept her voice low.

"We'll see," Tik said.

"What are you folks doing out on such a beautiful night?" Luis asked. He dropped his bedroll and a sack on the ground. "I've got some to contribute to the evening meal. And a little extra treat if you want."

He pulled a loaf of bread from the sack and followed it with a metal flask, the kind that usually held whiskey or some other hard liquor.

Mellow took the bread from him. "I'll soften up the jerky. We should finish off the apples and cheese we got at the last place. Thank you."

Luis smiled and gave a nod to her. "I haven't had fruit or cheese for a while, ma'am."

"Mellow," she said. "And that's Lena, Scott, and Tik. They usually have better manners."

"No need to apologize. The road is no place to be over friendly with strangers."

"You travel a lot?" Scott asked.

"All the time. Spend a day or two in a community now and then, but I like the road. Free to do what I want. No one to tell me I'm wrong. Not that I'm always right, of course. Been working my way around the country since the change."

"I used to do that," Scott said. "You get to know a lot of people wandering about. But it's lonely a lot of the time."

"Only if you let yourself feel what you're missing. And not as many travelers as right after it all collapsed. Most people have settled somewhere. I might join them when my body breaks down a bit more."

Lena let Scott lead the discussion. He was more like Luis than any of them. And he was careful enough with their own story that he wouldn't put them at risk. It gave her the opportunity to observe this Luis. If they could trust him and he was willing to join them, he could be valuable. He did seem honest, and friendly, but that could cover a lot of bad intentions.

14

Lena had the last shift just before sunrise. The plan was still to head to Sunny Meadows, and she'd spend the hours on watch thinking about Luis. He'd slept through the night, possibly not even aware someone had been watching him as much as the horses.

His stories had all been about odd communities he'd visited on his wandering. He'd been as far as Portland on both coasts. Meeting him here, in a megastore parking lot, felt too convenient to be unplanned. There were far too many places to camp around the area and this wasn't the highway, but a small side road. She would hold onto her suspicions for a while.

Scott woke first. "I'll get the horses ready," he said. "I'll make sure his has water and feed. What are you going to tell him?"

The decision shouldn't just be mine. "I think we'll be safer if we go separate ways. He came from the direction of Sunny Meadows. I'm really hoping he decides to keep going."

"Whatever you decide," Scott said. "We all talked about it when the shift changed. Not as a group, you would have woken if we did that. Tik told Mellow he didn't care what we did with him, but keeping Luis under observation would be easier if he stuck around."

"Tik's getting more suspicious of everyone."

"It's survival, Lena. Anyway, Mellow said we should keep him. She thinks he has information we need, but if you think it's too dangerous, then send him on his way."

"If only it was that easy," Lena said. "I don't know if we have a good option. I'll start breakfast before everyone wakes and starts packing."

Scott unrolled the waxed canvas bag they used for water and slung a sack of feed over his shoulder. "There's a tap on the side of the building. I'll check if it works. If not, I'll check the ditches."

Clean water wasn't always going to be easy to find, but that was a problem for tomorrow. Lena started the fire again to heat water. They would have tea to go with the food: dried fruit, oatmeal and a handful of nuts.

The water was boiling before the others started to stir. Mellow was the first. She decided to do one more pass through the RVs before they left since it was brighter now than it had been last night.

"Don't go into the store alone," Luis said. "Probably nothing left that isn't soaked in rat piss or infested with bugs."

Tik untangled himself from the blanket and took the bowls from Lena. He rationed out the supplies into bowls, then added enough water to soften the contents. "I'm going to check for facilities. Don't need to be perfect, but it's better than using a bush."

Luis dragged his saddlebag to the fire. "I might have something to make the food tastier."

He pulled out tiny plastic packs and handed them to Lena. Cinnamon and pepper along with a pot of honey.

Lena thanked him and sprinkled the spices and sweetness into each bowl. "Trail food isn't bad, but it's nice to have just a little variety."

"I go through empty houses. It's just me, so I only need a bit of anything I find. Try to leave what I don't need in good shape for the next person."

"Most people wouldn't think like that," Lena said.

"It's not as bad as you think. Mostly the assholes are in groups. They take everything they can carry and leave the rest out for the animals, bugs, and weather. I'm not sure it's on purpose, just thoughtless. Vermin get a good meal. Everyone else is left out."

That sounds pretty much the way the world worked before, Lena thought.

Luis tested the contents of his bowl. "Needs a few minutes. You got something you want to say before they come back?"

No point in denying it. "What are your plans?"

He kept his eyes on the soaking food. "You mean, am I planning to steal what you got and leave you stranded?"

"Not exactly," Lena said. "I mean, are you heading anywhere in particular?"

"No real plans. What about you?"

Lena explained her idea and then looked around. The others were still giving them privacy. "Sunny Meadows, then on west."

"I could help. I know where communities are. Know which to avoid. Know the places willing to give shelter or aid."

"Why haven't you settled down?" Lena thought about everything Luis had said or done while he was camped with them. He'd been generous with his supplies and entertaining with his stories. He said he was careful not to take too much or waste what he left when he scavenged. He could be lying, or just not mentioning some benefit he'd receive from being in a group for a while.

"Before, I was settled. Had a wife and kids, a good job — lawyer. Then the plague took it all. Never much liked rules. I get it, lawyers aren't known for their free-spirited approach to life, but I wasn't always one. Anyway, taking to the road was a way to reset my life. Then I liked it. Tried a few communities, but I kind of lost the skills of getting along with people and rules I don't like."

"It would be good to have a guide," Lena said. "Is there any reason we shouldn't take you into Sunny Meadows?"

"I just came from that place. If you let me hang out with you, I'll wait here. People in Sunny Meadows are nice enough, but they don't take too well to wanderers. They put up with me for a day or two to hear the news. If I don't have anything to tell them, they turn me away."

"Okay," Lena said. "We shouldn't be gone more than a day or two. So, let's agree to meet back up here in three days. Gives us all some leeway, and this isn't the worse place to wait. If we aren't back together by the end of day three, we all go our separate ways."

"Gives me some foraging time."

The others drifted back to the camp and Lena listened to their chatter. No one had objected to her decision, and she would be doing her research at Sunny Meadows. If Luis's story checked out, she'd be happy. If not, they wouldn't make the rendezvous.

15

Sunny Meadows was a pleasant enough community. Lena's group were welcomed and given shelter. The leader offered them some supplies in exchange for news and a few hours of hard work in the fields.

The residents didn't like Luis. When Lena asked about him, their guide tried to avoid answering. When she didn't change the subject, he said, "the man's useful for news, not that we crave knowledge about the world outside our walls. He likes it out on the road. We like it in here."

When Lena talked about her vision it didn't impress anyone, perhaps she should have taken the hint from the comments about Luis. Their welcome cooled after the conversation, nothing concrete, but a definite chill. The leader asked them to leave that night, adding, "We like what we've got here, and we plan to keep it just the way it is. You add strangers, you add problems."

THAT WAS A WEEK AGO. Since then, Luis had worked his way

into their trust, and a stranger would never guess he wasn't part of the original party.

He'd led them to three communities along the way and offered suggestions on how to approach the leaders. They hadn't had any success, but Lena learned more about how to tailor her words. Eventually someone would say yes, or at least a maybe.

"You give any thought to what happens if you don't convince more than one or two communities between here and the coast?" Luis asked as he added a new pressed log to the fire. Another surprise find in one of the cabins along a lake where they were now camped. "There's got to be a minimum for success."

"And it's going to be hard to sign other people on in the future if only a few get to make the agreements," Tik said.

Maybe that was why she was having so much trouble. Why would anyone agree to such a weak vision? And if she didn't have the basics down, it would take years.

"You were a lawyer, Luis," Mellow said. "Would you be willing to help with a document?"

Luis poked the fire again. It didn't need encouragement; it was the kind of thing people did to buy some time. Perhaps to tell the real story of why he was on the road. Perhaps to make up another lie.

"You know so many of the leaders," Scott said. "Maybe we should let you do the talking. Give Lena a chance to think about the future."

"Like a CEO?" Luis asked. "She does strategy, I take on the implementation."

"I think that might alienate more people," Lena said. "CEOs didn't have the best reputation before."

"Most of the people leading successful communities got there by surviving some pretty awful shit," Luis said. "I think

Lena's got to be the one selling the idea. Comes off more genuine."

"But?" Lena asked.

"It's too soon to sell," Luis said. "You're getting stuck because you can't answer the questions that come up."

"I've been told to back off a bit," Lena said. "I get it, but it's not easy to change."

Luis nodded, but he was still thinking. Lena kept quiet to give him time to make up his mind on what to say. She added water to the pot for more tea. Being inside a cabin, even one that smelled of mold and animals, was preferable to being outside. It gave them more time after dark to talk. The windows could be blocked to keep the firelight inside. And if it started to rain, they would be dry — until the roof started leaking.

"I wasn't the kind of lawyer you need," Luis finally said. "I did criminal law. Sure, I can help write up an agreement, but only trust makes it work."

"Who did you defend?" Tik asked with a sharp edge to his voice.

"I guess you've got a pretty good idea," Luis said. "Gangsters and drug lords. Didn't want to, but they threatened my family. And when I left Cuba on a tiny boat, it was because I believed in the American way. One of those things was that everyone gets a defense."

Tik stiffened, his hand reaching for where he normally kept his crossbow. "Yeah, so you work for them now?"

Luis flashed a look at Tik, then seemed to relax. "You have some history?"

"Not like you."

Lena glanced at Scott and Mellow. Mellow shook her head, as if to say they need to work this out. Lena hoped working it out didn't result in blood.

"No? You worked for them, right? They make you?"

Tik glared at Luis. "Just because they didn't threaten me doesn't me I had a choice. I did everything I could to protect kids from them."

Luis looked at the flames. "Right. I came from one oppressive regime to another. Started when I defended a junkie. The cops came down too hard. It was a solid case and I won. The next morning, I got pictures of my children standing on the porch of my house. Then I got called to a meeting. If I didn't work for them, my kids would suffer first. The kind of people who become gang leaders don't change. I guess you know that. You still work for them?"

"Never."

"And if they threatened to torture and rape Mellow?"

"I can take care of myself," Mellow said.

Luis nodded. "Tik knows what I mean. No, I don't work for any assholes. I stay on the road to avoid getting trapped again. The plague killed my family, but the gangs took them first."

Tik relaxed. "Yeah, I get it. They don't let go too easy."

16

"There's not much around here," Luis said as they camped for the night.

In the last couple of weeks, he'd introduced the group to four new communities. Each different, and no one turned them away. No one jumped on the bandwagon either. Lena had tried to modify her explanation, because the others all agreed she was going too fast. In thinking about how she would introduce the concept, she came to realize that it wasn't just a gut instinct; the area around the farm had become more stable when the communities agreed to work together.

At first it was only one, Prosperity. Then Newton Cole started his land grab. No one could fight him off alone. When they formed the alliance, they beat him. It didn't work so well when Poorjohn set up camp on her empty fields. The other communities were leery of going against the congregation that followed him. Was that the difference? Only an immediate threat could make people stand together? Lena hoped not, because it would be too late when the threat was on someone's doorstep.

In the last few days, the terrain had shifted from farm-land to a more arid desert. Large expanses of beige land with sage and scrubby bushes scattered across it. The change meant they needed to be more careful about water and food. Between here and the mountains of the coast was going to be weeks of this dusty landscape.

"You've been antsy all day," Tik said. "What are you hiding?"

Luis looked up from his plate of beans. "What are you're talking about? You think people stick around out here? Not much to support a handful of people, let alone a town."

Something in his voice made Lena sure that Tik's question hit a sore spot. Luis had worked his way into their trust and felt like he was part of the family. There was no way he'd managed to travel around for six years or more without running into problems. Why did he need to hide the story, or did he think they would turn him away for bad choices?

"Leave him alone, Tik," Scott said. "We all have private things. I didn't wander as long as Luis, but I made some mistakes. Places I wouldn't go back to, some who didn't want me back."

"Not always about what you did, right?" Luis said. "Someone needs a scapegoat, you're the easy target."

Scott nodded. "Once or twice."

Mellow dragged a branch from Angel's load to add to the fire. They'd stopped to chop firewood in the last camp where they'd had tree cover. The supply was dwindling, and soon they would need to forgo hot food until they reached a forest.

"The fire's high enough," Luis said. "Save it for tomorrow."

"It still gets cold at night around here," Mellow said.

"One more log and I'll soften the grains for breakfast and steep some tea we can have cold."

Luis's face tightened, then he gave his head a little shake. Whatever he was about to say he kept in.

"There's not much point in dragging it out," Lena said. "When we run out of wood, we eat cold rations, but until the last branch is gone, we should enjoy it."

"We have plenty of starlight for the overnight watch," Tik said. "No one can sneak up on us, it's too open. Maybe a pack of coyotes, but they aren't known for their stealth, right? A lot of yipping before they even get close."

The horses were hobbled close to the camp. The fire and presence of their people kept them calm. Lena looked up at the sky. The sun wasn't quite down, and yet, a few of the brighter stars were already showing.

"Maybe we should double the watch," she said. "It's not like we sleep that long. And we're not hiding from anyone." She waited for a reaction from Luis to her words, but he was deep in thought staring at the flames. "It'll be easier to stay alert with a partner."

Luis agreed to sit the first watch with Lena. Passing off to Tik and Mellow. The third watch would be Scott alone.

THE SUN WAS JUST CLEARING the horizon when Lena woke to the sound of voices. Not unusual, but this was too many men. She kept her eyes closed and her breathing slow, buying time to assess the situation. No sound from Mellow. That didn't feel right. She wasn't the chattiest person, but she wouldn't keep silent in a confrontation.

She cracked an eyelid. Scott was talking. Tik was standing alert. Luis was off to the side, trying to distance himself. Mellow sat at the fire, looking like she was tending the food, but her crossbow was within reach. A bolt in position. The conversation sounded calm, but maybe that was about to change.

"You must give us Luis," the older of three men said. The newcomers were all mounted, dressed like they belonged to a fundamentalist sect.

Lena slid her eyes to take in Luis. He was definitely ready to run. She unrolled from the blanket and stood. "What's going on?"

The man on the horse didn't acknowledge her.

Scott turned away from him and said, "They say Luis committed a crime and must come back to this place called Virtue to stand trial."

Luis kept his gaze averted. He hadn't run, and probably had the opportunity before the men arrived. No one could have snuck up on their camp while Scott was on watch. It put a mark on the positive for him.

"What is his crime?" she asked. It didn't matter that the man pretended she didn't exist. Scott would pass on the question anyway. Lena had no intention of validating the "only males get to talk" world view.

Scott turned to Luis. "Care to answer Lena?"

"It's a setup," he said. "I did nothing."

"You made a promise," the man said. "The girl is no longer untouched."

"The truth, Luis," Lena said.

"I didn't touch her, and I didn't promise anything."

She didn't want to ride with Luis unless this was cleared up. He was telling the truth; she held no doubt that he saw himself as innocent. But the men on the horses also believed they were telling the truth.

"Will it be a fair trial?" Lena asked, then waited while Scott translated her question into a male voice.

"The facts will be laid out. The girl will speak, and we will decide what his punishment will be."

So, no. "What punishment?" If they intended to hang Luis, or some other method of killing, she couldn't agree to hand him over.

"We do not decide in advance," the man answered Scott. "It will not be something he cannot pay. We ask that he face his actions, not give his life."

17

"Your women will stay in the barracks with the other unmarried," the lead man said. He was called Jacob and hadn't bothered to introduce his companions.

"They are our wives," Tik said.

Jacob turned in his saddle to stare at Lena and Mellow. Lena's skin crawled as his eyes travelled from her hat to her boots. "You have papers to prove your union?"

Lena had learned early in the day-long journey to keep quiet. When she or Mellow spoke, either Jacob ignored them, or looked at Scott like he should be better at controlling the women. She'd amused herself by occasionally urging Bebop closer to Jacob's horse, forcing him to trot to keep his distance. She'd stopped when Luis mouthed, "Stop."

It was petty of her to annoy the man who would mete out whatever form of justice he felt Luis deserved.

"Our word should be enough," Scott said, "since there are no authorities left."

"We protect the moral compass of our community.

Your women are not to be allowed to wander Virtue and corrupt the young. They will stay with the other unmarried."

Lena glanced over at Mellow, who was staring at her hands on the pommel of her saddle. A tiny smile curved the corners of her mouth. Perhaps it wouldn't be too bad hanging out with women until this was settled. Being able to talk and ask questions would give them more ammunition to fight for Luis.

She really hoped he was telling the truth because if he'd ruined the girl, as Jacob insisted on saying, she would leave him there to his fate. She might not agree with Jacob's beliefs, but this girl had to live there. And these kinds of societies didn't have much pity for women who'd made a mistake. Or if the girl was a child... She couldn't entertain that thought.

On arrival, an older woman dressed in black scurried from a long building. She beckoned to Mellow and Lena, then turned around.

"I guess that's our accommodation," Mellow said. She turned River toward the retreating woman.

"Your horses stay here," Jacob said. "We will care for them. The boy will come out when the women are gone."

"We'll see them settled," Scott said.

Lena slid from Bebop's back and unhooked her pack. Mellow did the same, adding the bag with the few books they'd picked up along the way.

"I'm already sick and tired of this," Mellow whispered. "Maybe we should wait outside this dump and let Scott and Tik take care of Luis's problem."

"Believe me, I'm tempted," Lena answered. "I need to know more about this, though. If Luis is able to travel with us from here out, I want to hear every detail."

"Are you going to dally out here all night?" the woman who'd come out of the building asked.

"No, we're ready. I'm Lena, this is Mellow."

"You don't use your husband's names?"

"Last names?" Lena asked. "No, we just go by first names these days. We don't come from a big place, so no confusion yet."

"Might have convinced Jacob you were married if you did. My name's Martha. Come on, I'll introduce you."

The barracks weren't just for sleeping. In the back, Lena saw a small kitchen where a kettle sat next to a fire, and mugs lined a shelf above a basin of water. Across from that was a walled-off room that was big enough to hold a toilet. The left side of the room held banks of bunk beds with curtains hanging down. The right side was lined with work-tables, some containing old fashioned treadle sewing machines, looms, and knitting projects, all with women quietly working. Life as it was hundreds of years ago.

"Are all the other women married?" Mellow asked.

"There are three more of these barracks," Martha said. "Married women stay with their husbands, widows here, girls live in their own building until they get married. More widows than new brides."

"All the girls get married?" Lena asked. "I thought we were going to stay with the unmarried."

"I decide where women live." Martha showed them to two bunks. "How else are girls going to survive without a husband? Men take on more than one if we have a surplus. What skills you got?"

"I learn fast," Mellow said. "I can knit a bit, but I'd love to weave."

"What if I don't have a skill?" Lena asked.

"Anyone can scrub clothes or dig compost," Martha said.

"Dinner is in an hour in the main hall. Figure out how you want to contribute while you're here before we turn in." Martha walked over to an unattended loom and started working.

"Where do you think we'll hear the most gossip?" Mellow asked as she tossed her bag on the upper bunk.

"Here. The work doesn't take much brain power. I'm guessing they do nothing but talk when there are no strangers around," Lena said. "We just need to get them to trust us. And I have a feeling these women know the most, too."

"They don't seem to be bothered about the men running the place."

"I'm bothered enough for anyone. We need to see this girl, and I don't believe for a second that all the women get married. What do they do with the women or girls that the men don't want?"

"Well, let's make ourselves useful. Everyone wants tea when they craft, right?"

Lena helped Mellow make the tea and then joined the women at the sewing machines. By the time they were summoned to dinner, both Mellow and Lena had met the women and picked up the basics of the work, and they were assigned simple projects for the next day.

Martha led them to a large barn where tables were filled with basic foods that smelled like heaven. "It's going to take a few days for the trial. Jacob is going to want to try to talk your men into staying in Virtue before they start the proceedings. He'll want to know how your men will react."

18

The days passed slowly. Knitting and weaving were useful skills, so Lena learned everything she could from Martha. The first day, no one spoke more than to offer tea or instructions. Neither Scott nor Tik visited. Martha laughed when Lena asked about the absence of the men.

"Why would they come? Jacob won't let you alone with a man unless he is sure you are married."

The second day, Mellow got her teacher talking about life in Virtue but it was all obedience and gratitude to the men so nothing useful.

"The deaths didn't change much," Martha said when Lena asked her about the history of the town. "The plague didn't pass us by despite our firm moral behavior. The leader then just closed us off even more. Saying that we'd been punished for letting outsiders in."

"And you just go along with it?" Lena asked.

"They hunt, and we farm and cook. They defend us and we behave." Martha stopped Lena from sliding the shuttle through the warp. "You missed a warp thread. Unwind and do it right."

Lena did as she was told and stopped asking questions. Martha had left something out of the history. There were too many women here for them all to be so compliant.

"I'll make a pot of tea," Mellow said. "To celebrate knitting my first scarf." She held up a pale cream object that could be a scarf, but it was far wider in some places than others.

"It's almost mealtime," Martha said. "Lena, you and Tess go bring the food here. We need to keep working."

Tess was a quiet woman, possibly in her mid-twenties or mid-forties — this life did harsh things to a woman's skin. She'd watched as Martha gave instructions on weaving, pursing her lips now and then as if she knew a better way and was afraid to say so.

The meal was prepared by a team of women and girls in a long, low building. Tess handed a basket to Lena. "Get the breads and meet me by the fire. We'll take meat and fruit back. Sandwiches are easier to eat while we work."

"You must make a lot of clothes," Lena said. "I didn't think there were that many people here."

"The men trade for things we can't grow or make," Tess said. "Just collect the bread and stop bringing attention to us." She walked to where a young girl was filling baskets with apples and pears.

Lena set three hearty loaves aside and picked up a knife to slice them.

"Let me." A boy of about twelve started slicing the loaves. "You being a stranger don't know the rules. Men use sharp knives, not women."

It was said without any accusation, but Lena suspected that the men didn't want to arm the women they treated like possessions. "Thank you. It's the first time I've been tasked to bring lunch."

He tossed the slices into her basket. "You'll learn."

His assumption that they were staying was a surprise. There was no way Scott or Tik would agree to it, no matter what would happen to Luis without them. She nodded and walked away. It was no use trying to change the boy's attitude. If no one living here challenged the status quo, then a stranger should leave it as it is.

Tess was waiting in line for her turn to receive today's protein. The fire was tended by two boys, and a man who must have been in his sixties sliced the cooked meat, showing an expertise that told Lena they'd had years of practice.

"What is that?" Lena asked.

"Deer."

Whoever prepared the meat did a great job with spices and herbs. It was hard to find actual spices these days, but much of the flavor could be mimicked by the right combination of local herbs. The aroma made Lena's stomach rumble. Sitting and working a loom didn't seem like enough to build an appetite, but it was hard work.

Their baskets full, Tess nodded for Lena to head back to the workshop. "No need to hurry," she said. "I want to talk where Martha can't hear us."

Lena slowed and moved beside Tess. "Okay." No one in the street seemed to be paying any attention to them.

"You need to understand that we chose this. People like Martha had a life before the plagues. The kids didn't, and most of the younger women had already signed up before the first sickness. Jacob wants us to keep as much of the changes out of Virtue. He says comparing doesn't help accepting."

"So, you all grew up in this…" she didn't want to label it.

"I know you think it's a cult, but it isn't. It's better for us to be subservient to the men than try to live outside the walls."

Not an argument Lena could win. "Everyone makes their own choices."

"Exactly."

"It's not all bad outside your walls, right? It's mostly people trying to survive."

"But there are bad people, right? Who do you think we'd meet? We're protected here. We don't learn the skills we'd need to survive."

"I'm not here to change you," Lena said. "We'll be gone as soon as the trial it over."

Tess looked at her and gave her a smug smile, like she knew better. "The girl. Jane. She wasn't born here. You say it's not horrible out in the world, but it is. Her parents sold her to Jacob. What kind of people do that?"

"Is that what she said?"

"It's what Jacob said, and she didn't tell us otherwise."

Lena didn't want to ask the next question, but she couldn't ignore the fact that everyone here called this Jane a girl. "How old is she?"

"When she came, she was eight or so. Now she's sixteen, most girls are a year married by that age."

"Her parents sold her before the plagues?"

"They were starting up," Tess said. "She doesn't fit in, but Jacob says we need to settle her. No one wants her now. Although, there wasn't a line of suitors before Luis got to her."

At sixteen, Jane was far from a child. Luis was still far too old for her, but at least it wasn't what she feared.

19

Another two days passed before everyone was summoned to the dining hall in the middle of the afternoon. The case was going to be heard and decided in one sitting. Lena hoped to be back on the road by morning at the latest. Her ability to show a meek face to the world was running out. She wasn't the only one. Mellow had snapped at Martha the day before when she was told to roll yarn into balls for the other women. Granted, Mellow's knitting had barely improved, and perhaps it was a better use of her hands, but it took a lot to make her react harshly.

Martha grabbed Lena's elbow and pulled her to a seat in the back row. "You sit with me."

Mellow joined a group of younger women and sat closer to the front.

"What's going to happen?" Lena asked.

"They'll bring the girl out. She'll tell the story they fed her, if she's smart. Luis will get a chance to answer the charges and then Jacob will announce the decision."

"It sounds like they've already decided. What if Jane won't tell their version?"

"Well, she's a stubborn one, so we might enjoy a show before Jacob gets his way."

"And what will happen to the girl?"

Martha looked at Lena, lips pursed. "I know you think we're stupid for letting the men behave like they run the place. It's not like that. Men like to peacock. Always have. Life goes much smoother if they think we're obedient. Mostly we make the decisions, just let the men think everything is their idea."

That made more sense to Lena than any of the stories about being protected. "This trial? You've decided what will happen?"

"We'll see how it goes," Martha said. "Pay attention so Jacob doesn't think it's necessary to ban us from the room."

Lena sat forward to hear better. The panel sat at a longer table facing the room. Scott caught her eye and turned away. She hoped it wasn't because he'd agreed to something she would hate.

Jacob sat in the middle, two men on either side of him from the community. Scott and Tik were positioned on either side of Luis at a table set to the side. Luis looked like he was going to bolt. She was looking forward to hearing what had happened to the men in the time they'd been separated.

"Bring in the girl." Jacob motioned to a side door.

A guard reached behind him and pulled it open. A girl stumbled in as though she'd been pushed. She was tall and rangy, long blond hair tied back in a braid, and dull brown clothes that seemed to be made for a larger woman. None of the attempts to make her dowdy could diminish the glare of defiance in her eyes.

"Repeat the details," Jacob said.

Interesting that he phrased it that way, as if, like Martha suggested, they had rehearsed her story beforehand.

"That man," she pointed at Luis, "led me astray. Promised me he would be my husband and abandoned me." Every word was spit out like it tasted bad. Lies, or perhaps not the whole truth.

Luis didn't look up. He'd given up looking for a way out and now seemed ready for his fate.

"Take her back to the penance house." Jacob waited until Jane was gone and then turned to Luis. "You were aware of our rules. Why did you violate them?"

Luis looked up this time. He paused and then stood. "I did not promise her anything. I did not touch her. She is still a clean, marriageable woman."

That also sounded rehearsed. Lena wasn't sure if she believed him because she knew him better than Jane, but when he told them his history, he'd been sincere. And he'd showed no behavior toward any of the women they'd met that would prove Jane's accusations. As much as Lena wanted to believe the girl, she couldn't push aside the thought that this court was simply theater.

Jacob called two people as witnesses to Luis's actions. Both men, they recounted seeing Luis walking toward the barn with Jane. But nothing solid enough that it had been improper, except that Luis was alone with a woman.

When the witnesses returned to their seats, Jacob stood and knocked on the tabletop. "The facts are before us. As is our custom, we will now adjourn to collect the thoughts of the community. Because of the nature of the charges, we will allow the man's companions ten minutes to discuss."

Lena shifted ready to join Scott and tell him her opinion. Martha touched her arm. "Wait."

"We have determined the following options to resolve

this," Jacob continued. "Luis must marry the girl regardless of the decision. Virtue has no place for a woman who has been soiled. Luis is welcome to join us here, as one of our citizens if he wishes to obey our laws. Luis can continue to travel and return to his wife here. We expect him to do so three times a year. Luis can take his wife with him on the road."

The crowd stood and gathered in small groups discussing Luis's fate. Lena caught Mellow's eye and nodded toward Tik and Scott. Luis was gone. Apparently, they didn't care for him to hear the conversation, or more likely they wanted to keep him from talking.

Scott drew them into a corner where they could speak without being overheard. "Well, that was a waste of time."

Lena nodded, glad she wasn't alone in thinking the trial was just a show. "What does Luis think?"

"He wants to get back on the road and never come back," Tik said. "That girl is setting him up. I believe him. She is rebelling against the men here. I'm guessing she saw Luis as a way out."

"I think Jacob wants her gone too," Mellow said. "Will he marry her?"

Lena chuckled. "I don't think he has a choice. Jane is the problem. I can't see her agreeing to the wedding."

"She will," Scott said. "Look, she wants out, and Luis is the easiest way. We've seen how they monitor the women. There's no way she can escape without our help."

"Her parents sold her," Lena said. "That's the story I got. So can you tell him to agree to marry her and bring her out with us. I don't really want to add a rebellious teenager to the group, but I can't leave her stuck here. This seems to work for most of the women, but her life will be hell if we abandon her here."

"Your time is over," Jacob shouted from the table. The room went silent.

Scott whispered, "Go back to your seats. We'll get Luis to do the right thing."

Lena sat beside Martha for the final words. The right thing wasn't that clear. If Jane was truly rebelling and using Luis for her own ends, was the right thing to make decisions for her?

Luis was escorted in and placed beside Scott. Jacob announced the options, this time with Luis leaving Jane with them while he wandered as the first one. The citizens wanted her to stay?

Only because she was looking did Lena notice Scott tap Luis when their preferred option came up — the last one.

"I'll marry her and take her with me," Luis said.

20

Their horses and supplies were waiting for them after the trial. Lena expected a wedding, but it seemed that Jacob, or perhaps Martha, wanted Jane gone more than married.

Martha told Lena as she handed her a bag of mittens and scarves that Jacob figured any guilt over Jane's fate was passed on to Luis. "That's what we all wanted. The girl gone without us taking any blame for what happens to her. Girl like her don't fit in a moral community like this."

Her words were so contrary to her earlier attitude, Lena wondered how much they'd been played. If Jacob had brought Jane with him and handed her over rather than bringing Luis here for the trial, he could have saved a lot of time. No one would have been happy, but they would be a lot closer to the coast than they were.

Now, they were on the road, putting as much distance between them and Virtue as possible. The camp last night had been quiet. No one wanted to talk about the experience with a stranger at the fire. They'd packed up and headed west as soon as the sun gave enough light to see the way.

Jane was riding Angel, and the packs were distributed on all the horses. A new horse was going to be a costly purchase. Perhaps they could get by without an extra. But it was a risk. If any of their animals was injured or sick, there was no replacement.

Luis pulled up beside Lena. "I'm not marrying her," he said. "We drop her off at some community that fits her personality, right?"

Lena shrugged. "I think we should let her decide. And don't worry, I have a feeling she was looking for an exit rather than a marriage. I think they went about it in the most awkward way possible, but Jane leaving was the end goal for everyone."

"Yes, she's had enough of people making decisions for her, but she might not know how to make a good choice," Luis said. "She wouldn't have had any opportunities to practice."

"She needs to start, and it's best she does it now," Lena said. "We won't let her do anything stupid. She needs us for survival right now. But I expect you to help teach her."

He glanced over his shoulder where Jane was riding next to Mellow. She'd changed out of the loose, dull garments last night and borrowed some of Mellow's clothes.

"I know of a market," Luis said. "We're going to need to outfit her."

A market would be good for all of them. "We don't have much to pay for supplies." Lena started making a mental list. Jacob had made it seem gracious that he wasn't going to charge them for feed and shelter. But now they had another mouth to feed, and supplies had been low before the detour.

"They have a labor plan," Luis said. "Most people don't have anything of value to spend or trade."

"We'll talk about it when we stop to eat. How far?"

"From around here? Half a day's ride. But we keep moving in this direction, we put more distance."

It was too early to stop to eat. Why did everything have to be irritating? She didn't expect the journey to be smooth, but nothing seemed to work out easily.

Lena stopped and waited for the others to catch up. There was a small clearing ahead. If it also had a stream, the horses could drink while they talked.

"You don't need to worry about me," Jane said. "I'm not soft like the other women back in Virtue. I come from warriors."

Lena suppressed a smile. Jane had grown up in Virtue; she had no idea what the rest of the world was like. None of them did. "I don't want you getting hurt, or worse. We're happy to have you with us until you find a better community."

"I am not marrying that man," Jane said. "You believe he didn't do anything, right? That I said what I did to get away from Virtue?"

"Yes," Mellow said. "Jane, we're not making you do anything you don't want to. We're trying to help set you up to survive."

"My name is Astrid Trygg. They stole me from my parents and tried to make me forget. But I remember."

"Martha said your parents sold you," Lena said.

"No. Three men came to my parents. We lived in a cabin in the hills. They wanted women, more women. At the beginning, they didn't have one for each man. My parents said no. They grabbed me at the lake the next day."

And probably not just her, Lena thought. Did Martha know the truth? Or was she maybe one of the women stolen like Astrid? Lena was surprised that she believed the girl so easily.

"Okay, you still need clothes, food and weapons," Scott said. "Can you use a bow?"

"I can learn."

Lena figured that if determination was the way to master a skill, Astrid would be self—sufficient before they knew it. "Are you willing to do your part? If we need to work at this market? We'll get you outfitted, and we need some supplies. Will you help us?"

"Yes. Warriors work together. I can protect you as we travel. Your journey works for me," Astrid said. "I want to travel the world, I mean, at least this bit of it, before I join any community. And maybe I just want to be alone anyway."

"Then we divert to the market," Tik said. "Not for long. We've lost too much time. I don't want to be stuck in the mountains when the snow hits."

It was beginning to look more like that would be a reality. Time slipped away. A few days in Beta, a week in Virtue, now some undetermined time at this market. It was still possible to make the coast if the weather held, but they needed to create a plan B soon.

"Let's talk about that when we're there," she said. "Luis, lead the way."

"We'll be inside by dark," he said. "No dawdling. Place is called Liberty."

21

L iberty was enclosed in a metal wall, like a few of the other communities. Lena understood the need for security, even if they didn't have it on the farm or the surrounding communities. There must be a lot of corrugated metal all over the country to supply the material. And you didn't need power tools to punch a hole for a bolt.

The rules to stay in Liberty were clear and uncomplicated. A list of items the vendors would take as payment, a list of jobs available to earn credits for payment. Cost of board. No fighting, no cheating, no stealing. It was after sunset, and they'd ridden all day. Lena was tired and afraid she'd miss some trick from this woman that stuck them here.

She ran some calculations in her head. They would need to be here for three days, use very little of the services, and then get out. If they stayed longer, the cycle of earning and spending would run out of control. Visions of their flight to the farm and eventual escape from Abigail's work-to-live rules made her determined not to be caught again.

She'd leave now if they didn't need supplies so badly, and to outfit Astrid.

"We'll take one tent," she said. "And where do we show up for work assignments?"

The woman at the entrance desk handed her a map and circled three locations. "The dorms are here. You talk to Benny. The work assignments happen at dawn in this tent." She pointed to the circle almost at the northern edge of town. "Be there early. Martin will sort you out. Basic food is given to you at work. You need more, canteen is here." She tapped a square building next to the dorms.

"Is Mickie around?" Luis asked.

"Usual place. Good to see you're still kicking, Luis."

"Takes a lot to bring me down, Eve." He turned to Lena. "I'll bunk with my friends. Hear what news they have. Let me know when you want to leave."

He hefted his pack onto his shoulders and wandered toward the sound of a party.

"Anything else we need to learn?" Scott asked.

"Your animals will be protected for free. Their food and any medical comes out of your earnings. We don't gouge. We want people to come and trade. If something happens to you, the horses are ours."

"Does something happen often?" Tik asked.

"People come here sick or hurt, we get the occasional asshole slipping past the gate. Keep to the rules. You'll be okay."

Mellow tapped Lena's arm. "Thanks, we should go now before we fall asleep on our feet."

Eve waved them away and shuffled the papers on her desk into a pile.

"Three days," Lena said as they crossed the now quiet

market space. "We need to make a list of the absolute needs and the highest paying jobs we can do."

"I'll do my own work and buy my own weapons and clothes," Astrid said as though she was doing them a favor.

"You'll contribute to the costs of being here, but I don't see any reason you can't buy your own stuff. We'll provision the group for our journey. Nothing we need should cost too much." Lena kept her eyes on the light ahead that stood at the front of the dorms.

"How much?" Astrid asked. "To contribute. I want to help with the provisions, but I need to buy everything."

Lena nodded at this statement. She was too tired to argue with the girl, but she'd decided to let her do what she'd announced as they rode toward Liberty. "We know. Let's talk about it in the morning."

THE TENT they were assigned was large enough for them to sleep and have a table in the center to sit and talk. The latrine was far enough away that its odor didn't carry, but close enough to use at night.

They had all crashed into sleep as soon as they laid out their bedrolls. Now, about an hour before dawn, Lena sat at the table and calculated the costs.

"How long?" Tik asked as he took the chair next to her.

"It depends on our jobs and the prices at market. If we keep every cost to a minimum, maybe three days. I'm concerned more about Astrid's needs. Weapons will be expensive."

"I'll teach her to use one of the spare bows we got from Da Vinci. Set her a budget. It's not like we can carry an armory."

The image of Astrid in full Viking furs and a brace of

swords on her back made Lena giggle. She glanced to where Astrid was curled up in her blanket. "I think that's the least she's expecting to buy. She has no skills. Let's keep her to some knives and leathers."

"So, what do we need to get for jobs?"

"The best pay is beyond our reach. And I don't want us taking on any peacekeeping roles. Too much chance to be hurt or hurt someone."

"Laborer? Street sweeper?"

"Not quite that bad. They barely pay enough to live on. They need some clerks and bookkeepers. Servers. Mellow can do some nursing. I could do some teaching. They have permanent residents with kids."

"We should get going," Tik said. "We want a choice so we can't be late."

As the others woke, Lena prepared the last of their trail food, saving them the cost of one meal.

THEY MET AGAIN AT MIDDAY, taking their free bread and cheese meal to a table inside the market.

"I'm set for three days," Mellow said. "The doctor said he'd need me more than that, but I wouldn't commit."

Lena had taken a job doing inventory in the warehouse. "I have to be reassigned tomorrow."

"Can we go shopping now?" Astrid asked.

They did need to find out what the prices were in the market. "Sure. We have a good idea what we can earn and some time."

"I'll see you back at the tent," Astrid said, jumping up.

"Wait," Lena said, "I'll come with you. We don't have a lot of time before we all have to get back to working. Let's make this a scouting trip so we don't have to run our purchases back to the tent before we report back to work."

Astrid was eagerly bouncing from foot to foot. She'd never had a chance like this before. To give her credit, she considered Lena's words. Then, slumping a little, she said, "Okay. I guess. Come on."

22

"I still have some credit," Astrid said. "What else do we need?"

It had been three days, no one had taken advantage of them, and their work wasn't onerous. Lena enjoyed the evenings when Luis would drop by with stories from his traveling buddies. There were some changes since he'd last traveled west, but not earthshaking ones. A few communities had sprung up, one had failed, and the others he'd already chosen for visits were stable.

They would leave tomorrow, before dawn so as not to accrue any debt — that started at first light. Lena's sack was stuffed with dried food, warm blankets and warm clothes. Astrid had given Lena a quarter of her earnings and declared the rest her weapons funds.

This was their last visit to the stalls that filled the central square of Liberty.

"I want to get a few medical supplies that Mellow asked for, but I think we've hit the maximum we can ask our horses to carry," Lena said.

Astrid looked at her clothes. She'd picked up some soft

leather britches and a fur jacket that added to her Viking appearance. Her pack at the tent held spares and a few linen tunics and pants. She wasn't bristling with weapons, and this was her opportunity to change that. Lena was as determined to keep Astrid from making mistakes as she seemed to be heading for it. A few weapons, only that. Too many would make them a target or seem too aggressive for a community to trust the group.

"What have you got so far?" Lena asked.

"Luis helped me buy more bolts for the crossbow. I got plenty for everyone. They aren't as good as the ones you got before, but we need extras. Luis said that was smart."

It was because Tik would add the entire batch to his store of bolts. Everyone had three to keep with them and use for practice. Each one was retrieved and checked for usefulness after each session.

"We need to make sure whatever you buy will be portable and can be stored," Lena said. "It looks like the vendors are in the far corner."

"I can do my own shopping," Astrid said, taking a step away.

"I think I can help you. Maybe negotiate a better price?"

"I watched Luis do it. I'll be fine."

Why was she trying so hard to get away? "You need skills to use any weapon, Astrid. Are you sure you know what to buy?"

Astrid firmed her lips and scowled. A perfect teenage response to an adult trying to help. She took a few more steps as if she was being drawn toward a specific vendor.

"I can learn to use anything," she said. "And I will practice. I promise."

Lena wasn't going to let Astrid go by herself. The town might be safe enough, and no one had been violent toward them, but people who dealt in weapons could be different. She wished she'd thought to have Luis help the girl; Astrid seemed to see him as a mentor. But her automatic response was to keep them apart.

Not because she didn't trust Luis. Astrid was her worry. She lied. Not the big one that got her away from Virtue. Lena could understand how she would do anything to escape. Astrid had told the truth as soon as they got far enough from her captors. The girl cast little fibs out like nothing. She lied about what she'd eaten. Not too much, but too little. Like being a warrior meant starving. She lied about how long she'd stood watch. Too long, in Lena's opinion. They would bring her out of that habit given enough time. It was possible that was her way to survive the oppressive environment. What concerned Lena the most was Astrid's blindness to her lack of skills with weapons.

She seemed to believe a little practice could give her mastery. She had no clue how dangerous a sword could be in an untrained hand. She seemed oblivious to the physical toll wielding heavy weapons could bring.

"I'm not asking if I can come, Astrid. I'm telling you. I won't step in the way unless I see someone taking advantage of you."

Astrid blew out a breath as if she couldn't be bothered arguing. "Fine."

Lena walked along the line of stalls scanning the wares. Astrid, her snit forgotten, pointed out the different killing devices.

"Do you want to look like you kill for a living?" Lena asked, trying not to tell Astrid not to buy a mace.

"You think I'm crazy," Astrid said. "I just want to look like I can't be taken by anyone again."

"Fair enough." Lena pointed to a set of knives. "You

could learn how to throw these pretty fast. And you can hide them in your clothes."

Astrid ran her finger down the blade of the smallest knife, taking care to avoid the edge. Lena wondered if she was trying to prove she could be careful. "I have a knife already."

So she'd lied when she said Luis had helped her buy crossbow bolts and nothing else. "I guess you don't care to show me what you really want. Is it something you think I'll object to?"

"You said you wouldn't interfere. Is that true?"

There was more to her story than being stolen and raised in a patriarchy. Someone had lied to Astrid enough that she didn't trust anyone. Lena wanted her to grow into a trusting but smart woman. No matter what she thought, she had to stand by her words.

"It is. I mean, I might have an opinion, but I won't stop you."

Astrid stared at her for a long moment and then nodded as if she'd made a decision. "Over there," she said, pointing to a stall in the shade of the large warehouse.

The vendor had a collection of weapons that must have come from a martial arts studio. Much of what was on sale here as weapons were things made since the fall. But a lot of the stalls, not only the weapons ones, had the spoils of a raid or scavenging trip. She saw samurai swords and staves along with some knives. The table held a stack of the collapsing batons that cops used, throwing stars were laid out on a cloth, and three sets of nunchucks. Other weapons she didn't recognize were piled in the corner.

"Which ones?" Lena asked, trying desperately to keep her voice from showing her fear. These all required years of training and were dangerous in the hands of a novice.

Astrid tapped a finger on one of the nunchucks. "I could learn to use these pretty fast."

"Have you seen anyone use them?"

"No, but I can figure it out."

"You'll hurt yourself badly," Lena said. "I don't think any of us have the skills to train you."

"I knew it. You said you wouldn't stop me." Astrid spun on her heels and stomped away into the crowd.

23

L ena rolled her blankets up and added them to the pile of supplies. The horses would be fine with the extra load. Most of it was food, so it would dwindle daily. The cost of a new pack horse was far too high for them to work for the credits. The tent felt less like home and more like a temporary space. It was a little damp and chilly since the fire had gone out. The slight odor of mildew was stronger, as if they'd left days ago.

"We can have breakfast before we leave," Mellow said. "It will take the last of our credits, but we don't need them after this."

"Good idea," Lena said. "It's a long way from our farm, but this kind of market is a great idea. Do you think we could set something up?"

"Hard to keep it honest," Tik said. "I talked to a few people, no one is thinking of opening more sites. But maybe if you get your way, we'll have a string of them from coast to coast."

Lena laughed at the idea of rebuilding what was essentially a big box franchise. "Not up to me, thankfully."

"I got a list," Scott said. "Things we can look for that will buy us credits on the way back."

"You think we'll come back this way?" Lena had imagined their return journey would lead them too far south to cross back to Liberty.

"Maybe. If we do, it would be good not to have to work," he said. "We can't always rely on having the skills they need. It's all small stuff, so we won't be burdened. And we won't sidetrack for anything. If we find something we take it, but no special trips."

"I think we should let Da Vinci know about this place. Even if we don't come past, a message wouldn't take too much effort."

Luis walked in with his pack over his shoulder; it didn't look any fuller than when they arrived. "He knows. They're coming up with an agreement to sell his smaller products."

"Did you pick up any supplies?" Lena asked.

"A bit. I got more information, and a few traps. Better to catch fresh meat, right?"

Lena agreed. Living off travel meat and bread was possible, but not pleasant. "What did you learn?"

He tossed his pack into the corner, his bedroll slipped out of the straps on the top. Luis grunted and secured his blankets. "Talk about it on the road? Unless you want everyone knowing where we're headed? Liberty is better than most places but you can't trust strangers with anything."

"Okay," Scott said. "Should we head for breakfast?"

Coming back to the tent after the meal might be a mistake. The sooner she handed the tent back to the manager, the better. "Let's get this all over to the stables. That way we're ready to go."

"Have you seen Astrid?" Mellow asked. "I know she went out a couple of hours ago."

"I thought she was going to check the horses," Lena said. "She took her supplies." If they had to spend time looking for the girl, Lena wasn't going to be happy. Any delay in leaving here was yet another day short for their journey to the coast.

Lena ushered everyone through the tent flap and sent them to the stables. She headed to the table set up for assigning shelter and told the woman that they were vacating. The woman insisted on inspecting the tent before she signed off. It felt a little like they didn't trust her to keep to the rules.

"Most people don't do such a good job," the woman said as if she'd read Lena's thoughts. "Mostly I got to clear out garbage. I get anything of value I find, but I appreciate a clean place better than some bits and bobs of trash."

In the old world it would be the other way around. Despite this being a marketplace, no one seemed to be trying to become rich. Just enough to get along, and a few little luxuries. How long before greed took over? Lena had no expectations that the answer was never. People were still people.

Lena hurried to the stables after the handover, wanting to saddle up and be on the road before they lost too much time. Breakfast would be fast, and they should be gone in an hour.

"She's not here," Scott said. "Astrid. They said she dropped off her supplies and said she was going back to get something."

"She had a few credits left last night," Mellow said. "She didn't see the need to hang onto them if she wasn't planning to come back."

Lena handed her pack to Luis. "I'll go find her. I think she might have gone back to the weapons dealers."

24

L ena walked through the market, which was quiet. Most vendors stayed closed until after the morning meals were done. Still an hour or more before this would be a bustling place with travelers and citizens alike bartering for supplies and goods. The weapons vendors were one of the exceptions. They would open at any hour if a deal could be made. If Astrid had returned after their fight, she could have arranged an early purchase. One that would ensure Lena couldn't stop her.

The vendor was open. Two young men were picking over the weapons laid out on the table. Lena scanned the contents but couldn't tell if one of the nunchucks were gone. The supply could be kept elsewhere with each purchase being replaced.

She waited until the boys had decided on their purchase, a single throwing knife, before approaching.

"Your girl came this morning," the vendor said. "Not enough for what she wanted." He grinned at Lena. "I put the price up beyond her credits. She would have damaged herself more than any opponent."

"How did she take that?"

"Pissed off, but she couldn't do anything to change my mind."

"Did you notice where she went? We're leaving today and I want to get going."

"That's not so great news," the vendor said. "There's some sellers in the market that don't register. They hang out in saloons and sell under the table. I saw her headed towards one of their places." He lifted his chin to point out a building in the shadow of the wall.

THE LOCATION WAS MORE than shadowed by the wall. As Lena approached the door, a damp cold wrapped itself around her. It felt like no one had passed this way for a long time. If Astrid was in here buying illicit weapons, they would have to move fast. To violate the rules at the very last hour in Liberty was stupid. The market was too valuable to risk being exiled forever.

She opened the door enough to slip through and closed it quietly behind her. The room was dim and as her eyes adjusted, Lena saw a large open space. A bar was against the left wall and what looked like the fire in a kitchen behind. Only one table was occupied. Two men, digging into a heaping breakfast of eggs and bacon. The shady business must pay well to afford them more than the oatmeal most people got.

"What do you want?" The question came from the bartender. He'd come in from the kitchen with a tray of clean glasses. He was tall and thin with lank hair tucked behind his ears. He put the tray down and reached under the counter for something. He didn't pull it out.

He was giving her the benefit of the doubt. The weapon he held would stay out of sight if he approved of her answer.

"A friend. She came here earlier. Young girl. Did you see her?" Keeping it short and to the truth might keep him from using force.

"Yeah. She talked to Ivan over there." He pulled a white cloth from below the bar and started polishing the first glass.

Ivan was finishing his plate of food when Lena stepped to the table. He was rough looking, most likely from spending too much time on the road plundering. His hair was cut close to his scalp, a scar ran down the left side of his face from hairline to jaw. He turned his head to look at her and Lena's gut went cold.

"I heard," he said in a raspy voice. "Your girl was here."

"Do you know where she went?" Lena wanted to learn what Astrid purchased, but it was more important to find her and leave than to be prepared for the fight that would come when they took her weapons away.

"Maybe." He looked at the other man and jerked his head toward the corner. "Private conversation."

The other man grunted and took his coffee mug away. Coffee, another luxury.

"Where?" Lena asked.

"Not in my interest to tell you," Ivan said.

"I just want to find her and be on our way."

"I don't know you. I don't know her. How can I be sure you won't go tell the cops?"

Was he looking for payment? He'd have to wait a long time because Lena had nothing to trade for information. Perhaps sending the men to deal with him would be better. But if he didn't think she was a threat, it might be an asset. Astrid might be a pain in the ass with her rebellion and determination to become a warrior overnight, but she was Lena's pain in the ass.

"You don't. How motivated do you think I'll be to keep your secrets if you help me versus if you don't?"

That raised a grin. "People don't threaten me," he said.

Changing direction might trip him up. "Did she buy anything?"

"That makes no difference to my answer. You think I have some kind of code about clients?"

"I think the answer is yes. You might not have a moral code, but you want repeat business, right? Selling to a girl too young to handle herself isn't great marketing."

"I don't care how capable my buyers are." Another grin. "Fair point though. The kid is going to get someone killed, but that's not my problem now, is it?"

"Yes, it's mine, and if I want her to kill someone, that's up to me. My group is getting on the road, we need her with us."

"I sold her some throwing stars. That wimp in the market is too careful for his bottom line. She had credits, I had merchandise."

Possibly worse than the nunchucks. "Where did she go?"

"Out the back door, like all the clients. That's all I'm saying. Leave before I call in a bit of reinforcement."

Lena peered into the shadows along the back wall. There was a door, but it was tucked into the darkest place between the dim lights around the room. She stepped toward the shadow, her hands reaching for a knife before she remembered the weapons were all back at the stables.

Through the door, Lena found a narrow alley between the back of the building and the wall. Only two ways for Astrid to leave. To the right or left into the market itself. The bright sun made her blink after the darkness of the interior.

Lena stood, waiting for her eyes to adjust. If Astrid slipped back into the market, she could be anywhere. The only two ways into and out of Liberty were under observation. Through the front gate where they'd come in, and through the stables.

It made sense that customers came this way. Any illegal goods would be easy to hide before they slipped back into the public areas. But what about large items? Surely there was a place to hide purchases.

She stepped closer to the wall and peered at the joins in the metal sheathing. It all looked solid, no secret exit from the market. If there was a way out, Luis or his friends might know.

Astrid didn't want to be found, or something bad had happened to her. For all her talk of a warrior heritage, she was still a child who'd been sheltered from the world. She'd shown many times that when she wanted something, she couldn't see anything but her goal.

They wouldn't be leaving today, or rather, they wouldn't be going far. It cost nothing to camp outside and walk into the market. Lena wasn't going to let Astrid be left behind no matter why she was gone.

25

"We'll camp near that turnoff," Tik said. "I'll keep watch for you."

Lena nodded because she couldn't trust her voice. Astrid's disappearance was tearing her apart. Somehow the girl had slid beneath her guard.

"We'll wait as long as you think it's worth looking," Scott said. "Come back to us every night, please."

"We can't afford to keep coming back," Lena said. "It's too far to walk, and I won't get stuck in debt for stabling the horses. We stay until we find her, or we have to give up."

Luis handed his pack to Tik and shouldered a smaller sack. "Lena, we'll find her," he said. "The damn girl can't have gone too far. When we bring her back, I'm tying her to the saddle."

"She's just testing her limits," Mellow said. "She's sixteen, and that's when a girl rebels. But maybe a bit of repercussion wouldn't go amiss."

"We're not her parents," Scott said. "We find her and if she wants to go out on her own, she just has to tell us."

"And we just let her walk away?" Tik asked.

Scott gave a small grin. "Well, she might make a different decision if we don't give her a horse."

Lena tried but found she couldn't raise even a weak smile. Everything Scott said was true. If Astrid had said she was leaving, or staying in Liberty, they would have tried to persuade her to stay with them, but would have let her go. Just leaving without a word was at best a childish stunt. At worst, it meant she didn't have a choice.

"Let's go back inside," Luis said. "My buddies won't be up for a couple of hours, but we can talk to everyone. I know this place, maybe I'll be able to tell who's lying about something important."

"Because everyone lies?" Lena asked.

"Yes."

Lena kissed Scott on the cheek and watched as the three of them rode towards the camp.

"Lena? We should get going," Luis said, touching her shoulder. "The horses will be fine in that cluster of trees just before the gate."

"We should start at the breakfast tent. She's always too hungry to miss a meal."

THREE DEAD-END LEADS, and it was already midday. Lena tried to hold onto hope, but she couldn't. Astrid didn't have the skills to stay hidden this well for so long. They'd followed her from the breakfast tent, where she'd eaten not long after the rest of the group. So, she didn't go missing from the shady vendor's place. Throwing stars could be hidden on her body, and if she didn't give anyone a reason to search her, the weapons would never be found.

The next clue led them to a clothing stall. Astrid had commissioned soft leather boots the first day they worked.

She'd picked them up and told the vendor she was rejoining her group. Was that a lie?

The final sighting was from a baker. Astrid had used her last credits to buy a bag of sweet fried dough.

"It doesn't look like she was planning on running away," Luis said.

Lena didn't want to give voice to the alternative. "Maybe she got hurt? Are there places she could go for medical attention other than the first aid tent?"

"Lena, face it. She was planning to come back to us. Maybe later than she knew we wanted to go, but she wasn't planning to run."

There it was. The scenario Lena didn't want to accept. If Jacob had come from Virtue to drag Astrid back, what could she do? "This place is supposed to be safe."

"And yet, she bought illegal weapons." Luis looked up to check the position of the sun. "We need to talk to my friends. If something is going on, one of them will know the details, or have a lead for us to follow."

Lena stood scanning the market crowd for a few minutes. She wanted to spot Astrid, or to delay the conversation with Luis's friends. Anything to put off the idea of backtracking to find the girl. Lena would not abandon her but rescuing her from Jacob again would put an end to any hope of reaching the coast this year.

"What if she was caught with the throwing stars?"

"She'd be in a holding cell. I have no idea what she bought from this Ivan character. Maybe he turned her away. People lie, Lena."

"I know that," she snapped at him. "It's worth a look."

Luis wiped his arm across his forehead to clear the beads of sweat. The day was hot, and the market was crowded. Lena's temper was fraying, and she was taking it out on him.

"It's over that way," he said, indicating a brick building next to the entrance to the market.

"I'm sorry," Lena said. "We'll find your friends next."

He led her toward the jail. "Just don't mention she has throwing stars or where she got them. Men like Ivan don't let informants live. Believe me, he's the kind of gangster I used to defend before."

Inside, a single guard sat at a desk. Behind him, a glass door showed a set of bars leading to a cell. The guard beckoned them over and pointed to the two chairs. "What can I do for you?"

Lena asked about any young girls who might have been arrested. "She's headstrong. Might be a handful to deal with."

"That young Viking in training?" He laughed. "Saw her yesterday all determined to get herself armed to the teeth. No, she's not here."

At least she'd made an impression, Lena thought. Luis thanked the guard and followed Lena outside.

"Your friends?"

"Let me do the talking," Luis said. "They don't like being questioned by strangers."

The friends were drinking at a bar, and looked like they hadn't stopped all night. Lena was happy to let Luis take over. She didn't have the patience to interpret drunk babbling.

Luis came to the point quickly. At first, no one was willing to say anything.

"Do I need to wait outside?" she asked.

The man across the table from her grinned, his teeth

stained with nicotine. "No. You stick around. Luis can wait outside."

"Just answer the question, Zeke," Luis said.

"Fine. You used to be fun, Luis. Heard Ivan made your girl come back for her purchase. You check the wall behind his place?"

"I did," Lena said.

"Not well enough," Zeke said. "Someone cut a gate in the wall. Did a good job of hiding it. That's how bad trade gets in, and sometime how bad trades get out."

THE GATE WAS obvious now that Lena knew what to look for, but if she hadn't been told, she wouldn't have found it. The edges aligned perfectly with the welded sheets, and it didn't go down to the ground. The bolts had been severed so they didn't go through but still looked right to the casual glance. Anything, or anyone, passing through would have to be lifted, including the gate, which sat in a channel and swung on a hidden hinge.

No sign of Astrid or any activity on the outside of the wall. No flattened earth from horses or people waiting. Someone came and cleared the evidence when business was completed.

"They cover their tracks," Luis said. "Patrols check the exterior daily, but on a regular schedule."

"Should we report it?" Lena asked.

"You want to find Astrid, or you want to be a good citizen?"

If the people running Liberty didn't know about the gate, then Lena was happy to keep them in the dark. She suspected they knew about it and made a cut on every transaction. "Astrid. We need to bring the camp here and start tracking her."

"I have a better idea," Luis said. "We can go through here back to the camp. I'll tell you when we're clear."

Lena peeked through to the other side of the wall. Nothing held the gate closed. So, the channels were the only security. A good bang at it would unseat the panel and reveal the violation of Liberty's rules.

"Why not go through the gate? It's closer to the horses and the camp." And she could take a side trip to tell Ivan exactly how she felt about him selling young girls, a lesson he would remember from the ache in his broken bones.

Luis looked over his shoulder and then nudged Lena to climb through. "If anyone noticed us come here, we're going to be detained. This way, we're out and free. And I know what you're thinking. Remember, Ivan has a lot of friends, and you have no evidence. So, you'll be in jail ten seconds after you try to land the first punch."

"I like that you think I could land a punch. I was just dreaming. Let's go."

He waited for her to land and step away before leaping through the opening.

"She's been gone a long time," Lena said as they jogged toward the small copse where they'd left their horses. "Won't wasting more time make it harder to track her?"

"It's been too long for regular tracking already. The people I'm thinking of are good at finding lost things. No matter how long they've been gone."

Lena saved her breath for running.

26

The delay from leaving by an unorthodox exit wasn't more than twenty minutes by Lena's internal clock. The camp was only a short ride at a fast trot. Luis made her keep below a gallop because he said the horses would need all their energy.

"We can track her while you go get your buddies," Tik said. "Mellow and me, we're good."

They'd been discussing the plan for an hour as they closed down the camp and got ready to move. The argument wasn't about going after Astrid, but about how to find her. Luis's contact was two days' ride away. Even pushing the horses harder would mean no sleep and a day and a half journey. By the time they found the trackers, Astrid could be too far to rescue.

"We shouldn't split up," Scott said. "This is going to cut into our journey enough, but at least if we're together we're all still heading west after we find these trackers. If we come looking for you, we'll be stuck in the mountains for winter. If we even get that far."

That was Tik's usual argument. Lena wondered why he was so willing to backtrack now.

"Scott's right," Luis said. "Remember, it's Astrid. She's not going to make it easy for whoever took her. We'll be traveling faster, and Kiaiyo's people know what's going on around here."

"So, they might already be aware she's missing?" Lena asked. It didn't make her feel confident. If they knew girls were being taken, they might be part of the organization doing it.

"If it's a gang, they'll drug her. Or beat her into going along. Or..." Tik shrugged.

"Or kill her?" Mellow asked. "Look, we could go after her, but I agree with Luis. We can't be separated. We go to these trackers and when they bring Astrid back, we continue riding west. Maybe we can make up some time by traveling the roads and not stopping for a few weeks."

Everything seemed aligned to stop Lena from making allies. But Mellow had a point, and they could make more contacts later on the trip. Lena refused to be forced off her dream of an alliance. Maybe she was crazy to think anyone other than her saw the benefit, but she had to try.

"If we leave now and ride through, we should make it late tomorrow," she said. "If Astrid is being Astrid, we can count on her causing trouble."

"We need to be careful," Luis said. "The road is pretty rough, so we can't ride at night. The days are long, though. We should be able to keep going until we can't see far enough ahead. We camp rough."

"So, who are these people?" Scott asked.

"The local tribes. What's left of them. Put aside their differences when the plague hit. Withdrew into the rez. Call themselves Nation One."

"Will they help?" Lena asked. "If they went off the grid so early, maybe they don't want contact?"

"Not survivalists," Luis said. "Kiaiyo doesn't let anyone join unless they have Indian blood. Although, I don't know how he can tell for sure. You probably don't understand what rez life was before, but it wasn't a big step for them to go off-grid. They weren't that far on."

"What if he says no?" Mellow asked.

"He won't. He'll push back but I know him. He sees helping out as the best way to keep his people safe."

27

They stopped on the flat top of a mesa looking out over a scene from an old western. The path continued down the side of the ridge, narrow and twisty. The main road swung to the side of the canyon, continuing south and west.

"Find some brush," Luis said. "The fire will get Kiaiyo's attention."

It was still light enough for them to have reached the bottom of the canyon, but Luis insisted the signal would be seen better from higher elevation. Lena hadn't argued. In the last twenty hours, they'd only stopped to water the horses and stretch the kinks out. Everyone was exhausted, and worrying about Astrid wasn't enough to keep them pushing on forever.

"There's no settlement in sight," Mellow said. She stood, hand shading her eyes, staring into the distance. "Are you sure we can be seen?"

"Probably being watched right now," Luis said. He took the branches from Scott and Tik, making a pile in the center of a flat rock. "Unpack enough to keep us warm but be ready to move when someone contacts us."

How anyone would see the fire at this time of day was beyond Lena. The sun was going to be down in an hour or so, but right now it was bright out. The shadows from the sides of the canyon were the only things giving depth to the landscape. She remembered hearing about the Grand Canyon. The way it seemed to call some people to step off the edge as if they wouldn't fall to their deaths. That was the feeling here. As if the ground was only a foot or so deep.

"Come back, Mellow," she said. "It's not safe."

Mellow leaned forward a little and then shrugged and turned back to the camp. "I thought I saw movement," she said.

"We should eat and rest," Luis said. "Take turns. People aren't the most dangerous thing out here."

"It feels clean and raw," Scott said. "Like everything is new and ancient at the same time."

"People would come to the desert to find themselves in the old days," Lena said. "I never understood before. But now? Scott's right. Everything is stripped away, but it doesn't feel empty."

"Vultures and scorpions," Tik said. "And rattlesnakes."

Luis grunted a laugh. "The vultures won't bother you."

"Unless the rattlesnake or scorpion gets to you," Tik said.

"We'll be okay until sundown. Then, creatures start looking for warm places to spend the night. Like your bedroll, or your boots." Luis finished tidying his fuel and pulled out his lighter. "I keep my eyes open for butane refills, but we won't find fuel for this anytime soon. Still, no point in wasting effort trying to start a flame the old way until we have to."

He held up a hand to test for the wind direction and beckoned them to move beside him. Then he lit the kindling. Within moments, a thick stream of smoke rose and flowed toward the canyon. "They'll see that and come running. Make sure we don't start a wildfire."

He'd build the fire with enough rocks around it to contain a spread. The smoke thinned but continued to rise. The only wildfire risk was if a loose piece of dried shrub tumbled through the camp and took flame with it. They could all keep their guard up for that.

"How long?" Mellow asked.

"No idea," Luis said. "We wait."

"I'll get some supplies out for food," Mellow said. "And the horses should be farther back."

Scott and Tik offered to help set up a temporary camp, leaving Lena alone with Luis.

"And if it takes days?" she asked. "We can't let Astrid be taken away."

Lena was overwhelmed with all the problems that seemed to pile on her since they left Liberty. Finding and bringing Astrid back to them. Keeping to a schedule that would make sure they were on the coast before the worst of the weather hit. Finding supplies to keep them moving. None of it was in her control, and all of it seemed like the most critical problem to solve. At some point, she would be forced to make a choice. Leave Astrid behind or give up on her desire to explore the country.

"I know. The more time it takes, the less likely you think we'll find her." He rested back on his heels.

"And you don't?"

"Sure, but I figure we've got time still. Kiaiyo's people are good, but that's not all of it. Tell me what you think happened to her."

Lena made herself comfortable on the hard ground. She'd spent the last two days worrying. Not analyzing or making up scenarios. If she really thought about it, maybe a shred of hope would make it through the fear.

"She was determined to pick up some weapons that we wouldn't have let her buy. To make herself more useful as a fighter, I think. She wouldn't have run away, even after we fought. Astrid knows we're her best hope to stay free until she can handle herself."

"I agree. She's pissed at the world, but she's sixteen and she's proven herself more than capable of manipulation."

"So, Ivan decides to sell her on," Lena said. "She didn't have much on her. Most of her purchases are in our packs. He most likely took whatever she had in credits, maybe anything else she had on her of value."

Luis nodded and put a handful of twigs on the fire.

"She would have fought," Lena said. "But not him. He wasn't hurt."

"I didn't notice any blood around that gate either."

"Drugged?"

"Maybe, but not for long. Carrying an unconscious prisoner isn't easy. A gag and some rope would take care of her."

Not for long, Lena thought. "Where would they take her?"

"That's the right question. Not too many places where you can sell people. I figure they won't go more than a week with her in tow. The longer they hold onto her, the more chance she has of slipping away or doing some harm. They won't be traveling fast, or for long, every day."

"Where, Luis? We can't count on Astrid escaping. Even if she does, how will she find us? And how will she survive on her own with no supplies or anything to trade?"

"Jacob wouldn't want her back at Virtue. I'm not saying

he won't keep taking young ones, but he likes his women obedient. There's a station a few days north. Train still runs to Canada — or did last time I was up that way."

"So why did we come this way?" She should have asked these questions before. They would have been at the station by now.

"Because it's not certain where she is," a new voice came from the path down the ridge. A man strode into sight. Battered straw cowboy hat on his head, long, gray streaked braid hanging over his shoulder. Maybe in his sixties, maybe older. Dressed in a faded denim shirt and jeans. "Luis."

"Kiaiyo." Luis stood and shook the man's hand.

28

"You need our help," Kiaiyo said.

"Missing girl," Luis said. "Would you like tea?"

Kiaiyo walked back to the trail head and said something quietly. He returned and agreed to take their offer of tea. Something about his actions told Lena this wasn't just a social nicety, but the opening offer in a negotiation. Lena was happy to let Luis take over because she had no idea how to read Kiaiyo.

Mellow handed Kiaiyo a mug of tea and then sat with the rest of the group around the fire. Kiaiyo placed himself across from Luis. "Your story? These people are new."

"You know me," Luis said. "I've been traveling with these companions for a long time. You can trust them like you trust me."

"Not saying much."

"Fine," Luis said with a sigh. "I got in some trouble over by Virtue after I left you last year. The missing girl is with us because of her own actions."

"Virtue is not a good place," Kiaiyo said. "Too many stupid rules."

"No argument here. The girl is young and not used to the real world. She's been missing for a couple of days."

"Time doesn't matter. If we agree to find her, we will." Kiaiyo turned and looked at each face around the fire, taking a moment to consider before moving to the next person. "I still need your story."

Lena tamped down on her impatience. Luis wouldn't have brought them here if he didn't think it was the best way to rescue Astrid. "We come from the east. New York upper state before. Now it's our farm, some nearby communities. Maybe a few more north and south. We rebuilt. Fought for our home."

"Why are you here?" Kiaiyo sipped his tea.

Lena explained her hopes to build some kind of connection with communities across the continent. "Not a new America, but something that will help us move forward."

"Why do you want to do that?"

Kiaiyo kept his gaze firmly on her face. No hostility, just focus. Lena hadn't settled that answer in her mind. When they started out four months ago, she would have said because it would make the world better and done it with complete confidence. Now, after meeting so many people with a different idea of the future, and hearing from her own friends that they didn't see the world the same way, she knew that was not completely right.

"When we were settled on the farm, or thought we were, someone decided to take it away. We fought and won but needed allies to do it. I think if we have some kind of common alliance, we can prevent power grabs."

"Lots of ways to protect yourself," Kiaiyo said. "Alliances don't always hold under pressure."

This wasn't the time to debate her ideas versus anyone else's. Astrid came first. When she was safe, or... Lena didn't want to acknowledge there was an alternative. "What's your story?" she asked. "You know what we're trying to do. What about you?"

Kiaiyo placed his mug on the dirt and leaned closer to the fire. A pack of coyotes started yipping in the distance. It was early for them to hunt but possibly things had changed for the local predators too.

"We got no help from the government when the plague hit. We lost so many of our elders and children. All the local tribes. Then the deaths stopped. We joined together and rebuilt our homes here. Not a reservation, our land. We don't take people in unless they have Indian blood. We patrol widely. No one is going to move us again. No promises to break. We don't need help from anyone."

Lena heard no anger, just firm statements. This time around, his people wouldn't be fooled into believing anyone.

"Okay, but Luis seems to think you can find Astrid."

"Your lost warrior?"

Lena smiled at the description, then realized no one had told him about Astrid's need to become more like her Viking ancestors. "You know who took her?"

"We've heard of these operations. They want to move across our land so they can get to their market fast, but we won't let them."

"How do you enforce that?" Lena asked. "Your territory is vast. Someone could sneak through without you knowing."

"Killed the first ones who came through. The captives were happy to spread the word about the savage Indians. We have patrols."

"And Astrid? How did you know about her?"

"Word gets through. You talk on the trail and don't think anyone is listening."

"Have you found her?"

"Come back to my camp. I have people looking, and we'll send more when you give them details about your girl."

"I thought you didn't accept people," Tik said.

Kiaiyo waved his hand to dismiss the challenge. "My camp is not near our home. We help people who need it, just don't take them in."

Luis stood. "We should get going before it gets dark. That trail down doesn't look easy."

Kiaiyo stood and dusted the seat of his jeans off. "Leave your stuff and horses here. I'll have someone lead them down. We'll walk. It's not far. If you knew what to look for, you'd be able to see it."

Lena glanced at Luis as they stood. Leaving everything to strangers felt like too big a risk. As much as she didn't want to ride down the side of the ridge on the narrow trail, she couldn't risk losing everything. Kiaiyo seemed trustworthy, but he was a stranger.

"They'll be careful," Luis said. "We'll be leaving a different way, so having our horses and supplies with us will be good. And I'm guessing that dinner will be worth the walk."

She glanced at the others. No one gave a hint that they were worried. Tik and Mellow shoveled sand over the fire and made sure the embers were buried. There wasn't much brush around, but it was all dry enough to catch easily. Scott shouldered his pack and held out Lena's.

29

The camp was only a short walk from the bottom of the trail. Lena looked behind her and saw three men leading the horses. All of them wore jeans and denim shirts along with straw cowboy hats in different stages of tatter. The lead man nodded to her and turned the horses to the right to follow a different fold in the earth. From her new perspective, Lena saw the ground wasn't flat as it looked from the mesa, but a cluster of canyons. The camp sat in a sheltered spot in the center, and the horses must stable inside the one to the right, based on the quiet neighs of welcome she caught.

This base was clearly temporary. Tents of camouflage fabric lined the walls of the canyon, maybe fifteen in total. A fire burned in the center of the space, no smoke rising. The aroma of grilled meat and spices reached out to greet them. Two women stood at the entrance to the largest tent, holding rifles but not pointing them.

"Scouts," Kiaiyo called quietly.

The two women stepped forward. They were dressed in a similar way to the men, but their hair was tied back and rolled into a low bun. They made no sound as they approached; the deerskin boots made it look like they didn't quite touch the earth.

"Tell them what you know, and they'll go find your girl. Then come sit at the fire." Kiaiyo walked away, talking softly to Luis as the others trailed them.

"It will be dark soon," Lena said. "When will you go out?"

"When you tell us about the girl and what happened. Dark comes faster down here, but it makes little difference to our work."

"Yeah, yeah. I'm Littleflower, this is Alice," the second woman said. "She likes to make it seem mysterious, what we do. But we mostly have clear nights, so the stars help, and the moon, while it's up."

Alice rolled her eyes. "I like a bit of mystery, so what?"

Now they were closer, Lena guessed the two girls weren't much older than Astrid. If she hadn't been taken by the men at Virtue, she would likely be much like these two. Unless her memory of her childhood was completely wrong, her parents would have trained her to survive.

"Thank you for trying to find her," Lena said. She told the two girls everything she knew. "She's tough, but I don't think she can survive out here without help."

"She'd have to be tough to find a way out of Virtue," Alice said. "That old bastard tried to take three of our girls a few years back. Learned his lesson, now he stays away."

The more she heard about Jacob's community, the more Lena wanted to burn it to the ground. But that wouldn't help her make allies and bring her vision to reality.

"Do you have an idea where she might be?" Lena asked.

"We don't work that way," Littleflower said. "If we follow the trail we think is there, we might end up losing time.

We've heard a few things that might help, so we'll keep an eye out for any signs of her as we backtrack to Liberty."

Lena wanted to ask so many more questions, but holding the two scouts here to satisfy her curiosity could make the difference between finding Astrid or not. "Good luck."

THE MEAL BROUGHT back memories of barbecues on the beach in Lena's youth. Vegetables and potatoes roasted in the fire; venison grilled perfectly on a spit. Cold tea was the only option other than water, but that just enhanced the flavors. It had been so long since they could eat more than just enough to keep going, that Lena couldn't stop picking at the scraps on her plate long after she was full.

"So, you are planning to make it to the coast by winter?" Kiaiyo said. "You find anyone willing to sign up to your alliance yet?"

Lena wiped the grease from her lips with her sleeve and put her plate down so she would stop eating. "Some interest, but I haven't gotten a yes."

"We're really just scoping it out," Scott said. "It's not a good idea to ignore the world these days."

"We had some trouble," Tik said. "People thinking they can just take what they want."

"I know what that's like," Kiaiyo said. "Had a few intruders ourselves since we gathered. Gotta deal with them, hope word gets out that you are too much trouble."

"Eventually someone with enough power will come along," Mellow said.

Kiaiyo nodded and sipped his tea. Lena noticed he did that, taking the time to think about what he was going to say before talking. She let him think while she tossed bones to the waiting dogs. A man took the plate away and refilled her tea.

"Not everyone is like that," Kiaiyo said, "but enough are. And they come from all kinds. Humans probably always dealt with power, greed. But we're good at keeping our home hidden, and we know this land better than any stranger."

"What did you do before?" Lena asked.

"Archaeologist. Mostly on my people's land. Finding and protecting sacred items. You?"

"Teacher," Lena said. "And after. But I couldn't stay in the town. Too many people wanting to rule over others. And the gangs were getting stronger." She didn't want to talk about what happened after they left. She knew the gangs took over, but it wasn't her story to tell.

One thing she'd observed as they passed through the towns was while the farm had its troubles, they'd been lucky. She didn't know for sure if it was because the land around them was productive, or other places were still easier to attack. The people who lived out here all seemed to have experienced multiple challenges and fallen to some awful times.

"And you want to bring people together? You don't think you'll attract more of the people you ran from?"

Lena drained her tea while she thought about it. "I never looked at it that way," she finally said. "I mean, I hoped we could build a defense against power grabs. You think I'm naive?"

He shrugged. "My study of history says yes. Every time something gains success, it attracts the people who will destroy it. Maybe it takes a thousand years, maybe only a few."

"I can't live that way," Lena said. "We're all too discon- nected to survive long. Like Mellow said, it won't be long before someone too big to fight will come at us. I know my solution isn't perfect, but it's something."

A shout came from the darkness at the edge of the camp, then someone swore. Kiaiyo stood, the men who'd been moving around in the shadows ran toward the noise.

30

A man held Astrid by the back of her jacket. She was fighting him every step of the way, but he skillfully dodged her attempts to wrestle free. Her hands were bound, but nothing else seemed to restrain her.

The man, like every other person in the camp, was wearing dusty cowboy clothes. Astrid had on her jeans and her fur jacket that was done up to keep her from slipping out. Her hair was tied into uneven, thin braids around her face, and tangled the rest of her head. She'd clearly been through a rough ride.

"Astrid," Lena called, "calm down."

She stopped suddenly, catching the man by surprise. He bumped her and staggered a little before regaining his balance. Lena suspected Astrid had a hand in the clumsiness.

"She wouldn't come with us," the tracker said. "Is she your lost one?"

Lena took a deep breath and nodded. "She's determined to take care of herself."

Kiaiyo beckoned them toward the fire. "You going to run?" he asked Astrid.

She struggled like she was trying to break the bonds on her wrists. "Not right away. You got some food?"

Lena closed her eyes in an attempt to calm her annoyance. They'd spent days worried that she was dead or worse. And here she was being rude to the people who saved her.

"We have food," Kiaiyo said. "You are welcome here tonight, but tomorrow you all head out."

The tracker cut the ties on Astrid's wrists with a flick of his knife. Astrid turned to him, swinging her hair like a threat. He stepped back, grinning. "Don't start what you can't finish, little one."

"I always finish what I start," Astrid snapped the words out.

"Mano, did you send the signal to the others?" Kiaiyo asked.

The tracker, Mano, picked up the broken zip ties and shoved the pieces in his pocket. "Deedee went to do that. She'll be here as soon as it's done."

"Come, sit and tell us what happened," Kiaiyo said. "A story before bed is always welcome."

Astrid sat and looked around. Her lips were cracked, she'd had no water for a while, and no hat to keep the sun off her face. The boy walked out of the shadows to hand her a plate of potatoes and meat along with a pitcher of tea and a cup. "Eat and drink slow at first," he said. "Don't want it coming back up. Waste of food."

Lena saw her struggle to follow his advice. Astrid glanced around and then poured a half cup of tea. At least she didn't fight everyone who tried to help, even if every movement and gesture screamed that she was only doing whatever they asked because she wanted to.

"I was getting away," she said. "They took me from the market. That asshole Ivan stole my credit and then didn't give me what he agreed."

"Did he take anything else?" Scott asked.

"No. I left everything with you guys." She tore the meat into small chunks and bit into the first one, chewing slowly and then washing it down with more tea. "Did you just keep going? Or did you look for me?"

She's just a kid, Lena reminded herself. "We looked. We found the hole in the fence. Luis brought us here to get help. What happened after they took you?"

"Assholes were going to sell me. Some train is working between old Canada and here. Said I was going to like my new job in some town." She took another bite.

"Mano? How did you find her?" Lena asked.

Mano took a drag on a cigarette he'd lit from a branch at the edge of the fire. "We heard about the train a while back. Chief sent us to scope it out. I guess we'd be shutting them down, taking what we could use. But I saw this kid sneaking behind a tent at the rail station. She thought she was clear, but the head guy was coming for her. I dragged her out and to safety."

"Yeah. And then he tied me up. Threw me on his horse and took off. What was I supposed to think?"

"I told you what I was doing." Mano took the last drag and tossed the butt into the flames.

"Yeah, and you couldn't be lying, right?"

"Astrid, didn't you listen? You were about to be caught," Mellow said. "Is there any place she can wash up?"

"Yes, but wait until you are ready to go. We can't waste water here, so you get one bath," Kiaiyo said.

"I heard what they said, but Jacob said he rescued me, too. I prefer to do my own saving, thanks."

A woman stepped into the circle and sat beside Astrid. "You can thank us any time, now you believe that we didn't kidnap you."

Astrid washed down the mouthful of potato and wiped her lips on her sleeve. "Fine. Thank you, Mano and Deedee. I would have been okay, but I guess we'll never know that now."

"No," Deedee said. "If we weren't there, you'd be halfway to some whorehouse. Being strong doesn't mean doing everything yourself. Let people help."

Astrid grunted in what could be agreement, or just resignation. She'd cleaned the plate and almost finished the entire pitcher of tea. "Thanks for the food. I didn't get fed."

"We'll send you on your way with some dried meat," Kiaiyo said.

"Um. How about I stay?" Astrid asked. "I need training. You could teach me all kinds of fighting, right?"

Kiaiyo looked to his right where someone moved in the shadows. He nodded and a woman around his age stepped forward. She whispered in his ear and then stepped back.

Lena waited for Astrid's reaction to what happened. Having been at the camp for a short while, she knew there was nothing subservient in the woman's behavior. The men also waited for Kiaiyo to acknowledge them. Astrid didn't show what she thought on her face. Good, perhaps she was learning the wisdom of keeping her thoughts inside until she understood the situation.

Kiaiyo stood and patted the dust from his jeans. "No one from outside stays. Mano, show them to the visitor's tents. My wife has suggested I give one of our horses to your young warrior. I know how challenging it can be to train one like her without breaking that spirit. Perhaps a feistier horse will help her."

31

"Astrid, please get your ride under control." Luis snapped out the words as Raven, the horse Kiaiyo had given to Astrid, came too close. The animal needed a firm and consistent rider, Astrid had not mastered either of those skills.

In the two weeks since they'd left Nation One, Astrid had taken her weapons lessons seriously. Between the group, they all had some wisdom to offer when it came to bows and knives. She'd insisted on standing early watch every night, and frequently didn't wake the next person when her shift was over. The constant double guard session left her tired and irritated.

Astrid nudged Raven and pulled on the reins gently to move him away. "He won't listen to me. Maybe he should be the pack horse and I can ride Angel. She's a better horse."

"Raven will end up running away with our supplies," Tik said. "He's small and fast, meant to be ridden. You know what to do, Astrid. You need to be more patient and focused with him."

Astrid grunted and guided Raven to the side of the road. "When are we camping?"

There was no point in arguing with her. Either she'd master the horse or end up falling on her butt enough to learn her lesson. "We ride until dusk," Lena said. "And tonight, you sleep."

"You need me to keep us safe," Astrid said. "You don't know who is going to try to steal our supplies."

"If you get a good night's rest, you'll be able to manage Raven better," Mellow said. "We can handle security for a while. We need you ready to fight if something goes wrong."

The flattery seemed to have its intended effect as Astrid stopped struggling for control and shifted her posture to use her knees to guide the horse.

Dinner was going to be a challenge. Even with the supplies from Nation One, they were running low. Beans boiled with dried meat for dinner, and leftover beans for breakfast. And the bags would be empty in a few days. Astrid's imaginary raiders would come away with nothing if they attacked.

"WE NEED TO TALK," Lena said as they ate the last spoonfuls of their dinner.

"I'll sleep," Astrid said. "Why do you keep nagging me?"

Lena took her last mouthful to help hide her smile. Teenagers didn't change no matter what the world was like. She chewed and swallowed. "Not that. We need supplies. And we need to figure out how we manage through the rest of the trip. I didn't think it would be so hard to keep our food going."

"I was expecting to hunt, or fish, or maybe set a few

traps," Tik said. "But we don't stay anywhere long enough for us to top up."

"Luis, you said you know this area," Lena said. "Should we camp for a couple of days? Maybe find a place with a river or something now we're getting closer to the mountains. Or is there a settlement around where we can trade?"

"Camp for a few days would be good," Luis said. "I can train Astrid with the horse; I got some tips from Kiaiyo's men last time I visited. We won't be able to dry meat in a few days' stop, but some fresh food would help. Cooked will keep for a day or two."

"And a settlement?" Scott asked. Lena hadn't missed Luis's lack of information, but she was glad of the reprieve from being the only one demanding answers.

"Not every community is safe," Luis said.

"And not every one of them is dangerous," Tik said. "Look, I'm happy to keep moving and stopping here and there for a few days of provisioning, but that's not why we're here. We want to find out who's out here. Learn who's on our side and who's a threat."

A slightly different take on her purpose, Lena thought. She understood Tik's priority was much like Astrid's, being prepared to fight off threats. Was she alone in wanting to learn about more than dangers? "Just tell us, Luis. Let us decide."

He gathered the plates and started cleaning them without answering.

"We can eat less," Mellow said. "It's the horses I'm worried about. We mainly sit all day. They have to carry us and our stuff."

"Getting out of this dry region will help," Scott said. "We'll find more streams and grass soon. The horses will be fine. We can't eat grass."

Lena watched Luis's back as he completed the chore. No one had forgotten the question, but they were all giving him time to think about his answer. Was he cooking up a lie, or trying to get comfortable with telling them the truth as he saw it? She couldn't make a decision without information. He had the expertise and she valued it, but not to the extent that he could decide where they would go without consultation.

He packed the dishes and wiped his hands on his jeans. Then his shoulders squared, and he reached into his bedroll, bringing out a flask.

"We might as well finish this," he said. "One less thing to weigh us down, and a good storytelling aid."

They each had a sip of the... perhaps whiskey or vodka — the taste was the raw burn of alcohol, so it was hard to tell. Luis put the cap on the flask and tucked it away. "I know of five places within a day's ride. Or at least there were a year or so back. Two are north, we'll have to come back here to keep heading to where you want to be on the coast. One is a day's ride back, and the other is ahead, just in the foothills."

"Why didn't you take us to the one we passed?" Astrid asked.

"Last time I was there, things were getting weird. If they survived, I don't know how they'll react to strangers. Maybe welcome us, maybe shoot us on sight."

"What about this one ahead?" Lena asked. "Are they likely to let us work for supplies, or take something in trade?"

Luis stared off into the darkness beyond the fire. He didn't respond for a long moment. Then he nodded his head once. "They are different," he said. "I won't go in with you, but I'll wait a little farther along the road."

"Different how?" Lena asked.

"You'll see. I think you'll be fine. Probably will let you in. They have supplies and need some strong backs now and then for labor. Just keep your wits about you, and don't believe everything you're told."

32

"You follow that trail," Luis said.

They were gathered in front of a stone arch with the words "Live Right" carved at the top. Over the last two days, the landscape had gradually become greener, the ground rising into low foothills. Trees blocked the view on the side of the road, and a stream ran beside it. They'd fished and eaten well, but now their supply bags were empty, and Lena worried over the cost of filling them.

"Where are you going to camp?" she asked. "I'm hoping we'll be fast."

"There's a rest stop a mile or so along. I'll be waiting for you," he said, pointing. "Don't count on getting much for trade with your magazines and books."

"It's all we have besides labor." Scott was looking up the trail. "How long will you wait?"

"A week, maybe ten days. Then I have to go on. It's still a long ride to the coast. I'll have time to hunt and cure some meat, so you won't have to trade for that."

A week or ten days was too long, Lena thought. "If we are late, we'll catch up."

Luis looked over Lena's shoulder. "What is that girl up to now?"

Lena turned to find Astrid standing on the path, reaching toward a clump of bushes. Before she could ask, a rattle sounded and something darted out of the shade and attached itself to Astrid's hand.

Tik jumped to the ground, pulling a knife from his belt. He yelled at Astrid to hold out her hand and sliced down, separating the rattlesnake from its head.

Astrid squeezed until the fangs released her hand and then screamed in pain.

"Take her to the people up there," Luis shouted. "Move fast. They can deal with it."

Tik held Astrid in front of him on Storm while Scott grabbed Raven's reins to lead him. "Mellow and Lena, ride ahead," Scott said. "Tell whoever you see what happened so they can be ready."

Lena urged Bebop to a canter. Mellow was behind her as they passed the rest of the group. A gallop would be faster, but not knowing the terrain made it too much of a risk.

"Come in, be welcome." When Lena and Mellow reached the gates of Live Right, a woman waited. She was thin and her face was stunning despite the harsh angles. The makeup she used to soften her features was obvious but didn't detract from the overall image. She wore a simple sun dress with thin shoulder straps; it was gold and looked like it was made of silk.

"Our companion was bitten by a rattlesnake," Mellow said. "We heard you have medicine. Can you help?"

"Of course we will. I am Nicolette Light, and you are?"

Her voice was soft and gentle. She held out a hand, but not to shake, more as a blessing.

Lena introduced herself and Mellow. "The other three of our companions are close behind. Scott, Tik and Astrid. She is the one injured."

"I hear them coming. Four horses?"

"We have a pack animal," Lena said.

Nicolette pulled a small bell from her pocket and rang it. A young man wearing a white linen tunic and pants ran from a gatehouse beside them. "Siren, please alert Doctor Moonlight that he should expect a patient, snake bite. He will know what to do."

The young man bowed with his hands together at his forehead, then sped away.

"Thank you," Lena said.

"Please come with me, one of our members will greet your party and settle them in."

"I would like to wait for them," Lena said.

"It will be better if you come now. This area is narrow, and we don't want to be in the way. I assure you the two men will join us. And your injured friend will be helped."

Lena dismounted and led her horse behind Nicolette as she escorted them to a stable block. A girl dressed in heavy homespun took Bebop and River in hand.

"Everyone looks so pretty," Mellow whispered as they gathered their packs. "Is that weird?"

Nicolette was speaking to the girl about the rest of the animals, far enough away that Lena couldn't make out the words.

"Yes. I mean the kind of pretty, right? Not natural? Most people these days don't bother with beauty products, but so far everyone looks like they've just finished a spa day."

"We value our skin here in Live Right," Nicolette said.

"People will be glad you noticed. We believe the soul shines in beauty. We don't judge others for believing differently. As long as their opinions don't intrude on our community."

There was a boatload of judgment in her tone, but Lena needed her help, so kept her response inside. "Riding all day for months tends to toughen everything," she said with a smile.

"Your companions are approaching," Nicolette said. "When they are settled, we will take you to the clinic. Then I think you would like to settle in. Healing will take a few days."

"Thank you," Lena said. Time for talking about trade and the cost of this kindness would come, but not until Astrid was on the way to healing.

The stable hand took the rest of the horses into stalls and said she would check them for injuries. No one seemed to think she was worthy of introductions. Lena couldn't help but feel like this place had a strong hierarchy, with Nicolette much higher up than anyone else.

"Thank you," Mellow said to the girl. "I've been watching for any signs, but I'm not an expert."

The girl nodded, glanced at Nicolette and then walked back to the stalls.

The clinic was a small building with four rooms set aside for patients. Lena scanned the locked cabinets filled with plastic bottles, medical equipment, and boxes of dressings, nothing she didn't expect to find in a clinic these days. The walls were decorated with posters of before and after pictures. At some point before, this must have been a place where people came for cosmetic surgery and recovery.

The doctor was another beautiful man. He smiled at them and gestured for them to join him in one of the rooms. "It will be a bit crowded, but I think Astrid will appreciate the company. But only a few minutes, please. She needs rest."

Inside, Astrid lay on a bed with an IV in her arm. "Hi," she said. "They gave me a shot and I'm kind of sleepy."

"Don't excite her, please." Doctor Moonlight stepped back and closed the door.

"There's something wrong here," Astrid said as soon as the door closed. "We should have made Luis tell us more."

"We kind of got sidetracked," Tik said. "Maybe you'll learn a lesson from this about not touching things."

"Yeah, yeah," Astrid said, her voice getting slower and quieter. "But be careful. That doctor creeped me out. And why are they so happy to use up medicine on strangers?"

Her eyes closed and her breathing became steady.

33

"I'll leave you to Siren," Nicolette said the next morning. "He will be your guide and introduce you to our ways. Ask him any questions you have." She turned and walked away, her long linen tunic making it look like she floated.

Siren was the young man from last night. He looked angelic, maybe in his early twenties or late teens. Blond curls touched his shoulders, eyes a deep blue, perfect teeth... it all seemed too polished for the world today.

"We'd like to see Astrid," Mellow said. "I don't want her wondering where we are."

Siren smiled and gestured toward the clinic building. "Of course. Our doctor will give you an update, and I can assure you she is getting the best care available."

That didn't mean much these days, Lena thought. The level of care was low tech and mostly natural medicines. "You do seem to have a lot of the old medicines and procedures," Lena said as they followed Siren along the path.

"Nicolette was prescient. At the beginning of the great cleansing, she called all of her followers to the spa. She purchased everything we needed. She invited natural healers with knowledge of plants. We have been safe here. None of our people fell to the diseases."

He said it like he'd rehearsed a script. Was Nicolette recruiting? It made no sense. No matter how much she stockpiled, the supplies would only last so long.

Scott put his hand on Lena's back like he wanted to remind her not to argue the point with the boy. "That's not something all communities can claim."

"Before, Nicolette insisted that her followers were healthy. All vaccinations, healthy diet, exercise. We committed to living long, productive lives. Here we are." Siren pushed the clinic door open.

"Good morning," the same doctor greeted them. "Your friend is doing as well as expected, given her general health."

"We've been on the road for a long time," Mellow said. "It takes a toll, but she's young, strong, and determined. My experience tells me she has everything it takes to survive."

"You are a medical practitioner?"

"I was taught by a nurse," Mellow said. "I know how to cure or heal most things that happen."

"We prefer to thrive," the doctor said, "but let us not argue. Conflict can affect healing."

Nothing he said was wrong exactly. Lena had seen enough people force their way through sickness. But stubbornness hadn't helped any of the billions who died. Everyone they interacted with so far had that smug attitude. Nothing overt, but the whole vibe was 'I'm better than you, you can't help it'.

"Can we see her?" she asked. "Just to set our minds at ease."

"She is sleeping, but certainly. Perhaps only one or two of you?"

"We'll wait," Scott said, stepping closer to Tik.

Astrid was covered to her chin with a cream-colored blanket. Her eyes were closed and her whole body relaxed. If only she could find some of that peace when she was awake, Lena thought.

"Should she still be sleeping?" Mellow asked.

"We have medicated her. A snake bite that severe is hard on the body, and in one so young, on her psyche. They tend to think themselves invulnerable at that age, don't you think?"

"Astrid in particular," Mellow said. "How long will she need to heal?"

"You are anxious to leave, I understand. It will be a few days, but she will have healed when we wake her. The wound as well; you don't want an infection to take hold when you are far from help."

"How long?" Lena asked.

"A few days. I can't be more sure than that."

"Will you show me the bite?" Mellow asked.

The doctor gently pulled the cover off Astrid's arm and turned her hand over. The bite wasn't bad, but streaks of red spiked toward her wrist. A pen line touched the edge of the longest.

"The streaks are not growing, so we are past the danger point. When it fades, and the bite is healed, she will be safe to travel."

"We'll see," Lena said. "Our group isn't planning to stay long."

They rejoined the others in the lobby. Siren suggested they tour the gardens. "Then we'll stop for some refreshments."

"I'd like to check on our horses," Lena said.

Siren's smile faltered for a moment. "Of course. Perhaps this afternoon?"

THE PEOPLE WORKING the gardens were another set of beautiful bodies. This time twins, a boy and a girl. Both had vibrant red hair cut in a bob to the shoulder. The only indication that they worked outside at all was the dirt on their gloves. Lena thought they might be around Siren's age, but it was possible they simply looked far younger than their years.

"Everything is organic," the girl, Amy, said. "Of course that must be true everywhere by now. Unless someone is manufacturing the poisons used in the past. We have to test each field we clear." She gestured past the trees lining the garden.

"There are stockpiles," Mellow said, "but we don't need to produce at the scale I hear was needed before."

Amy nodded and offered them a handful of blueberries. "Just harvested. Nothing tastes better than fresh fruit."

The berries were tart and not as flavorful as Lena remembered. "Wild?"

"The bushes don't travel well," Adam, the boy, said. "We are working to improve the fruit, but really all you need to do is bake them in a pie with enough honey and they are delicious."

"We will be late for lunch," Siren said. He ushered them back to the path and toward the dining hall where they'd been fed before.

. . .

"YOUR FRIEND IS HEALING," Nicolette said. "Our doctor tells me she will be ready to travel in a day or two."

Lena put blueberry jam on her granola, which was offered as dessert. "We would like to contribute while we're here. Perhaps trade for some supplies?"

"We could use some help in the fields," a woman at the end of their table said. "Maybe clear another section?"

"Tabitha, that is a wonderful idea," Nicolette said. Her expression didn't match the words. She wasn't happy to have anyone take over, although not much affected her pleasant expression. "Are you feeling up to that?"

"Our home is a farm," Scott said. "We've done it before."

"Then it's settled. As to trade, we don't have much beyond our own needs, but perhaps we can offer some dry goods. We will talk about this when you are ready to leave."

The conversation was finished. Lena asked about their horses again, but before anyone could answer, she felt herself slip away.

34

Lena blinked her eyes open. She was in her room, alone. The sheets were cold where Scott slept. She got dressed and checked herself in the bathroom mirror. Something was different. Her skin was smooth and not wind- and sun-roughened the way it had been yesterday. Falling asleep over lunch was probably going to cause problems, but she'd been so tired from the weeks on the road.

The dining hall was only half full when she entered. Astrid sat next to Mellow, both eating from bowls of what looked like oatmeal. Both looked rested and happy.

"You got out of the clinic way faster than expected," Lena said as she slipped beside them.

"Really? I feel great," Astrid said. Her smile was broad and, for anyone who knew her, disconcerting. Someone had taught her to braid her hair, and it was up in a complicated pattern.

"That doctor is a miracle worker," Mellow said. "Show Lena your wound."

Astrid held out her arm. The only evidence she'd been

bitten was the bite marks. The angry red lines were completely gone. "He said the holes would fade to nothing."

Lena waved away the server who offered her a mug of tea and a bowl of cereal. "I'm surprised you didn't want to keep the scar. I thought warriors were proud of their battles."

"Who wouldn't want to look their best?" Astrid returned to her breakfast.

"Where are the guys?" Lena asked.

"Working the field," Mellow said. "It's almost cleared. I'll need to meet the doctor soon for my shift."

"Doesn't he have a name?"

"Yes, Moonlight. I don't know why I call him just the doctor. Astrid has been learning in the kitchen. Apparently, no one in Virtue thought to teach her the skills she needed to be a good wife. I guess they hoped someone would take her away all along."

"Wait, the field is almost cleared? How much could they do in a few hours?"

"We've been here for three days," Mellow said. "You've been helping make jam and pickles. Wow, you must have slept really well to forget that."

Three days? No way would she forget three whole days. "One day, Mellow. We had lunch, I fell asleep and woke up. One afternoon and one night."

"I have to go," Mellow said. "I'll mention this to Doctor Moonlight, perhaps you've hit your head?"

"I'm heading over to start making stew for lunch," Astrid said. "Don't forget, Nicolette wants to see us later."

Lena was alone before she could ask any other questions. She didn't have a head injury because there was no pain. She wasn't hungry, so she left the hall and walked to where Amy had indicated the fallow fields were.

. . .

SCOTT AND TIK were working with a horse-drawn plow on the far side of the cleared area. The furrows closer were fresh and supported Mellow's statement. This was a farm before, Lena thought. Mature trees bordered what looked like two acres of arable land. Wind breaks like those around the garden.

"We will plant winter wheat."

Siren had come up on her as she watched the men work. "It's a bit early," she said. "We don't plant that at the farm for another month."

"The seasons come earlier here," he said. "Did you sleep well? I thought you might need an extra hour but when I checked, you were already up."

She needed answers, and Siren would not tell her if he thought Nicolette would disapprove. She still didn't understand how the three days had disappeared from her memory, but she believed that three days had passed from all the evidence around her.

"I need to talk to Nicolette," she said. "I think we need to agree on what supplies we can expect when we leave."

"She wanted to speak to your group," he said, "to offer you all a place here."

"I'd like to talk to her first," Lena said.

Siren glanced out over the field. His expression remained pleasant, but his posture stiffened. He wanted to say no. That Lena should wait until Nicolette was ready for them.

"I promise it's important that Nicolette and I reach an agreement before she talks to the rest of my group. And if they want to stay, I won't stop them."

He relaxed a little and turned back to her. "Then we should go to her office."

"Lena, I see the treatments are working," Nicolette said. She sat behind a large desk with an open journal. "You look ten years younger already."

"I'm sorry, I don't remember the treatments," Lena said. "I need to speak to you in private."

Nicolette's smile widened and she dismissed Siren with a wave of her fingers. "We are alone. How can I help you?"

"What did you give us on the first day?" She had no doubt that her memory lapse was due to some kind of drug. "My friends are not acting themselves. I don't have any memories of the last three days or any sense that something is missing."

"Sit," Nicolette said. "You are right. It's nothing harmful, I assure you. And as you can tell, it wears off if not constantly refreshed. It's an herb."

"You drugged us so we would work for you?"

"No. You were all very stressed from your journey. It was to relax you, to give you a chance to recover. I assure you nothing nefarious happened."

"You have a very different definition of 'nothing' than I do." Lena clenched her hands in her lap where Nicolette wouldn't notice the tension in them. The woman was not going to show any emotion and certainly no remorse. If Siren hadn't let her sleep, she wouldn't know anything about it. Luis would give up waiting, and no one at the farm would have any idea where they ended up. "This must stop now. And no one will make any decisions until they are sober."

"I thought you would let them make their own decision," Nicolette said. "Is that not true?"

"They won't be making their own decision until they are drug-free." Lena forced herself not to raise her voice. "If anyone wishes to stay, they can. But I will be leaving. I will expect you to provide us with a week's supply of untainted trail food. We will leave without delay. How long before the drug wears off?"

Nicolette stared at her, but it held no threat, possibly because her face couldn't form any expression but pleasantness. After a long few moments, she nodded. "I will instruct the kitchen to provide food to them that isn't enhanced. I expect they will be sober within a couple of hours. Once we have the discussion, I will provide the supplies you asked for."

"You gave in quickly," Lena said. "How do I know I can trust you?"

She laughed. "Because you are not the kind of people we want in this community. You care nothing for your looks. Anyone who decides to leave, I will be happy to have them go. But you will take Siren with you. Like you, I want to learn more about the country. To be able to anticipate enemies, or friends." She stood and held the door open for Lena to leave.

IT WAS late in the afternoon when Lena and her entire group mounted up. Nicolette had done as she agreed about supplies. Siren was astride a pale horse called Olive. Angel was laden with packs, and each of them carried a pair of saddlebags to lighten her load enough to keep her moving fast. Siren had clipped a pouch to his belt before mounting.

"We need to go," Scott said. "I want to get to Luis's camp before dark. I don't trust that woman not to come after us."

They walked the horses through the gate and down the trail to the main road.

"Lena," Siren said. He maneuvered Olive so he was beside her. "I was not given a weapon. Do you have one I can borrow?"

"Do you know how to use any?"

"I will need training," he said. "I must tell you that I did not agree to Nicolette's plan. She should not have drugged you. She wouldn't have done it last year, but she has been changing."

"Is that why you let me sleep this morning?"

"Yes. I will return, but with the hope things have not gotten worse in my absence." He unclipped the pouch at his waist and nudged Olive to the side of the path. He emptied the contents on the ground and rejoined her. "I will not require the drugs she sent along."

35

The next morning, Lena sent Siren to check the horses and gathered the rest of the group together. "He can't hear us. How are you all feeling?"

"Clear," Scott said. "I can't believe she drugged us."

"We're good as well," Mellow said, leaning into Tik's side. "She didn't lie about how long it would take."

Luis kicked dirt over the remnants of the fire. "You should have listened to me."

"You didn't say she would drug us," Tik said.

"I didn't know she was going to," Luis said. "I told you to keep your wits about you. And didn't the fact that I refused to go in tell you something?"

"We didn't have much choice," Lena said. "Astrid got the help she needed, none of us were permanently damaged."

"Yeah, so Astrid needs to be more careful. All of you do. Keep yourselves from needing anyone like that," Luis said.

"I'm right here," Astrid said. "And I'm sorry. And I'll be more careful."

"Well, Nicolette isn't the only one who'll do whatever it takes to keep people safe. I don't know all of them." Luis pressed his lips together like he was trying to stop words from escaping.

"Yes, we don't expect you to be familiar with every place," Lena said. "I don't want to waste time hashing over what happened. We need to talk about Siren. I agreed to take him with us, but I don't trust him."

"You think he's planning to trick us into going back?" Tik asked.

"Nicolette doesn't want us back," Lena said. "We'll never fit in, and eventually she'll run out of drugs to control us. I think she's using us to protect Siren while he gathers intelligence for the cult."

"You want to ditch him?" Luis asked. "We should do it soon, so he can find his way home. I don't like the idea of leaving him where he doesn't have the skills to survive."

What happened in the last few days to make Luis think that plan would be acceptable to anyone in the group? "I don't know what we should do, but I'm not considering anything that puts him in harm's way. Any more than we are by traveling at least."

"We take him along," Astrid said. "We train him to use the bows. Maybe training with him will be fun. We watch him. But we don't want to give him any weapons just yet."

"We search him," Mellow said, "before we go. I know he dumped a bag, but that could have been anything. And he's been alone with the horses. And we make him taste anything from the supplies Nicolette gave us."

"Good thing we kept watch," Lena said. "We don't have to go through all of our packs."

Luis separated the packs into two groups. "He could have messed with that pile," he said, nodding to the three bags he'd placed to the side. "They were within reach all night and no one would have noticed him if he shoved something in."

Luis had hunted a few small animals, but the meat was already gone. Without time to properly cure it, Lena had designated it as breakfast. She had no intention of staying so close to the Live Right property now they were free. "Okay. If we don't find anything, we accept him without suspicion, right? Otherwise, we send him back. I don't want to be worrying about Siren the entire trip."

"I'll get him," Mellow said.

Luis went through the three packs while they waited, finding nothing unusual. He sorted out the bags of food from Nicolette and arranged them on the outside. "We should make him taste everything when we stop for the night. No point in carrying this stuff if we can't eat it."

Lena hoped the food was clean because they would still need to find supplies if not.

Mellow led Siren into the camp. "The horses are fed and watered," she said. "We can pack and go pretty fast." She glanced at Lena and gave a quick nod. Lena hoped it meant she'd checked the animals for interference.

"Siren, we want to search you and your supplies," Lena said. "There's no point in pretending we trust you. You know exactly why we can't take the risk."

"I don't want to go back," he said. "I mean, I guess I have to go back eventually, but I want to see what's going on. Nicolette doesn't let us hear about the world. It's not that I don't trust her, but... I guess I don't, really. I want to believe she's looking after the community but without knowing, it's hard to be sure."

Nice words, Lena thought. He strikes me as someone adept at telling people what they need to hear to trust him.

"Then you'll be happy to know we'll trust you when we've searched you."

"What about making him try all the supplies he brought first?" Astrid asked.

"That's not about trusting Siren," Scott said.

"She wouldn't have tampered with the food," Siren said. "If she wanted you punished or drugged, or dead, she would have done it right away. But I'll taste everything."

He nudged all of his packs toward the women and then stood with the men for his body search.

Nothing appeared to be a problem. Siren did have a few small bags of herbs, but they were easily identifiable by aroma and shape. "He can prove these are clean when he tastes them tonight," Mellow said.

"He's good," Luis said. "We should go."

They attached all the packs Angel could manage and still keep up, again each of them carried some of the supplies on their own horses. The weapons they had were hung from their saddles. Siren was the only one who had no bow or knife.

Lena held Bebop back to allow Luis to lead them to the road. Scott joined her, guiding Beauty close.

"Are you satisfied?"

"What we saw was good," she said. "What about you?"

"You know how they all looked like models?"

Lena nodded. "I figured they did a bit of cosmetic surgery."

"Only on the parts anyone can see," Scott said. "Someone has beaten that kid. Old scars. I don't know if it was done at the cult, or before. Maybe the reason he joined. But I don't think they have the tools to remove the damage."

Lena couldn't believe Nicolette would cause damage to anyone — pretty was her thing. "Did you ask him about it?"

"We ignored it. Questions like that need a lot more trust than we have with him right now. But we will. Even if we can't do something about it, we need to be sure what he went through."

Abuse like that in his past made the boy unpredictable, but Lena wasn't willing to let Siren stay vulnerable. "And he gets trained to fight back, right? Not just weapons, hand to hand."

When they stopped for a break to rest the horses, Lena checked the saddlebags were secure. Since the trip to Nicolette's compound, she wasn't going to risk getting so low on supplies. Losing a pack would be more than just a problem.

The sky was dark with clouds; they would be soaking before they camped for the night. It meant finding another abandoned service station so they could be under a roof in the storm. As much as they wanted to make up time on their journey west, they would be forced to take the first shelter they found. The season was turning, making it less likely they would be in control of their progress.

"Luis, I don't want him here." Astrid's whisper was harsh. "He'll do something to harm us, or he'll hold us back so that woman can catch us."

Lena stopped moving. The two of them were just on the other side of the horses. She needed to hear Luis's response. Astrid had seemed to accept Siren. That's who she was talking about, surely.

"The boy is coming with us," Luis said, quietly. "Why the change of heart?"

"I was pretending. Lena thinks he's on our side, but they drugged us. Luis, we can't trust anyone from there. Our group should stay small, not add someone every time we stop somewhere."

"You think he'll take attention from you when we start training," Luis said.

Did he know nothing about teenagers?

"No. I learn fast. He's trouble."

"So are you," Luis said. "I'm not going behind anyone's back to get rid of the kid."

Astrid blew out a big sigh of frustration. "Why won't you believe me? You weren't there when they did that to us. You don't know what it's like to find out you've lost days."

"You didn't give anyone a choice because you poked that rattler."

"That's not fair."

"The only person who's caused trouble is you," Luis said. "I guess I can understand how you used me to get out of Virtue, but you don't listen. You walked into that situation in Liberty, you got bit by that snake."

"Yeah, I learned my lesson." Astrid's voice was rising and Lena could hear tears coming. "It still think he's dangerous."

"Well, maybe you finally got your warrior instincts going and found an easy target. You need to give the kid a chance to prove himself. Or you can talk to the others and do this in the open," Luis said in a tone that meant the discussion was over.

Lena stepped around Bebop and moved toward Astrid and Luis.

Astrid froze and then smiled like nothing was wrong. "Oh, I thought you were cleaning up with Mellow."

"Luis is right," Lena said. "We are keeping Siren with us." She was careful not to mention the boy's scarring. Astrid could take that as weakness.

"I told you," Luis said.

"That's not helping," Lena said to cut off Astrid's retort. "Luis, can you keep this between us? I don't want Siren thinking he's not wanted."

Luis nodded and then left to go back to the camp.

"But he isn't," Astrid said.

"You were excited this morning," Lena said. "You told me it might be fun training with him. What happened?"

"Maybe I was pretending before."

"No, you aren't that good at lying yet."

Astrid blinked in surprise. "Oh. Fine. On the way here, he was talking about his life in that place. If I'd been treated like that, I would have found a way to leave, maybe take a little revenge as I escaped. He doesn't care, even seemed happy about it. That isn't right."

The two young people had stayed together throughout the day. If something was wrong with Siren, Astrid was the only one who would discover it. She might not know about the scars, Lena thought. "You have no idea what happened to drive him to Nicolette. What exactly bothered you?"

"He didn't think it was wrong that you were drugged."

Lena tried not to agree with Luis, that this was jealousy on Astrid's part. "Really? Siren made it possible for me to wake up sober. You'll need to be really sure of your suspicions. Is there more?"

"He said you'd agreed to do the work to pay for supplies. And that's all that happened while you were at Live Right. The drugs made you happy. You just don't remember."

That was worrying. "Things are different all over now," Lena said as she worked through her reaction. "He is looking at it from a different perspective. Remember, Nicolette has been in control of him for a long time. There is a difference between knowing what you are doing and being unable to say yes or no because of someone's influence."

"And I learned something in the clinic," Astrid said. "I didn't realize what it meant until I knew what she'd done to you."

Lena's memories were slowly coming back to her. Doing the work for the most part, nothing worrying or traumatic. The drugs seemed to muddle more than just her mind; it made it hard to form connections. "Tell me."

"I looked at the books in the clinic when they left me alone. I guess I wasn't sleeping the whole time. I looked up snake bites. It takes months to recover. I'll be tired more until I build up my stamina, but we could have been on the road days earlier."

"And you think Siren had a role in keeping us in the cult?" Lena started to feel a little of Astrid's concern. If she wasn't drugged the entire time, she would have been looking at the same kind of books. Even if she'd trusted the doctor completely, a medical book would have given her and Mellow tips on all kinds of treatment.

"You don't?"

"I'm watching him, Astrid. We all are. I'm not saying I blame him for anything that happened, but we're not naive about the risk."

"Then we should kick him out."

"If we did, how would we be sure what he was up to?" Lena asked. "I don't want him to know how you feel. Can you pretend to trust him?"

Astrid's expression was all frustration and anger. Then she relaxed the tension and nodded. "If you think it's best."

"Keep your eyes on him while you're both training. If he slips any time, it will be then."

37

L ena rolled out of the sleeping bag. There was a chill in the air, not the kind that came with a rainstorm, but the kind that held a little bite and a promise of winter. It was only the end of August, maybe the beginning of September. They weren't so specific on the farm nowadays, but since they'd started through the mountains, it was clear summer faded faster than on the flatter lands.

"We'll stick around for a while," Scott said. "Let the day warm up a bit. Give us time for a weapons lesson with the kids."

Astrid and Siren had been training every evening when they camped. Lena could see Astrid's improvement after each session. Siren wasn't taking to it so well, receiving the brunt of Astrid's sarcasm after every missed target. "Not too long," she said. "I'll get breakfast going."

"Luis is already at the fire. We'll need something hot when we're done." Scott headed toward the clearing where the horses were hobbled, and they'd cleared some room for training.

The supplies they had from Nicolette were holding out well. Oatmeal with some dried fruit would sustain them until they camped again. She washed her face and brushed her teeth with a little water from the bucket set near the fire to keep warm enough to use.

Luis was poking the kindling to encourage a few more flames before adding a branch. Mellow and Tik were nowhere to be seen.

"Just us?" she asked as she placed the sack of oats next to an empty pot.

"Tik and Mellow went to check the traps we set up last night," Luis said as he jammed the iron frame over the now blazing fire. "If we caught anything, we can roast meat for eating on the road. Maybe get a little farther by not stopping for long breaks. Tea will be ready soon."

"We need to stop somewhere for a few days soon," Lena said. She filled the pot with water and placed it to the side of the frame next to the kettle for tea. "I don't think we should try for the coast in one go. Too risky unless we have way more supplies than we can carry."

"I agree. We can still make it, but things are different in the mountains. No gas stations to scavenge or use as shelter. Well, none close enough to be useful. You don't want to be riding into some of the old small towns that used to be around here."

"Abandoned?" A small town might be their only choice if the weather turned bad.

"At best," Luis said, "and nothing left to scavenge. Others? Let's say they make Virtue look like a beacon of freedom and equality."

In the background, the sounds of training floated to them. This time Astrid must be showing Siren her skills in hand-to-hand combat.

"You think Siren is going to be able to learn to fight?"

"That's another thing. That girl needs to train with people who are better than her. She's too confident. Siren is no competition, makes her think she's some great warrior. Kiaiyo shouldn't have said she was in front of her."

"To be honest, I think she'll get there no matter who trains her." Lena added oats to the boiling water and then dried cranberries. "So, do you know anywhere we should go? Maybe spend a few days resting and planning the rest of our journey?" She wasn't giving up on her dream of a united country, but they hadn't met anyone even slightly interested in weeks. And Nicolette was not her idea of a trusted partner.

"Yes. There's a place. Not sure how they'll feel about taking people in, but it's a fort. Lots of ex-army and wannabes."

"That would be good for training," Lena said. "Maybe we can trade some of the extra crossbows." They'd been careful to collect the bolts after using them, and thanks to Da Vinci's people, it was rare that one bent or broke. "Or we offer to work?"

Luis looked toward the training space. "Here's the thing. You know anything about the kind of people who set up survivalist camps before?"

"You mean preppers?" Lena stirred the mush in the pot. "We all thought they were crazy. I guess some of them knew what they were doing."

"These guys were set up by a bunch of religious types. Last time I visited, I heard a lot of preaching about hellfire and holy vengeance. You think you all can take that?"

The kind of people who weren't exactly open-minded about anyone who wasn't a believer, or was different, or spoke out or anything that didn't fit in a narrow definition of normal.

"How bad? I mean, we've accepted most of the different communities we've encountered. I haven't wanted to join any of them, but even Nicolette kept her people healthy and safe."

"I'm worried about Astrid and Siren mostly," Luis said. "You think she can keep her opinions to herself?"

"We'll ask her."

"Siren? We don't know if he was sent out to find more pretty people to join Live Right." Luis said, bringing up the idea he'd hinted at before.

And he hadn't been with them when they met other communities. "I have no idea. Again, we can ask. Although I think he is steady enough to keep his mouth shut. Astrid will struggle."

"I still think it's the best option," Luis said. "How about you and I head in when we get close and decide if it's worth the risk?"

"Reconnoiter? Maybe. How far is it?"

"A hundred miles? We don't go far in a day now. Depending on the weather, two weeks if we don't get rained in somewhere." He poured hot water over the tea and herbs in the pot and gave a sharp whistle to bring everyone to breakfast. "If it doesn't work out, we move fast to the coast, right?"

"Anything else I'm missing?" Lena asked. "I don't want a repeat of Nicolette's place, where we didn't understand your hints."

"No. If they bring you in, they'll keep their word. You might have to listen to a bunch of preaching, but they don't want new followers. Too many mouths to feed, and strangers might ask too many questions."

Lena thought about their supplies. They would just about make it and once again be delayed finding enough food to finish the journey. There was nothing they could do about it. Perhaps the preaching would come with a side of charity.

38

L ena thought back to the early days of the journey. Travel hadn't been all that easy, but the roads were clear and other than that one instance, they were able to see anyone who approached. Now, in the hills, it was all she could do to look up from Bebop's mane. The roads were uneven and narrow. Trees grew over the path, forming a dimly lit tunnel. And even hours after the rain stopped, drips from the branches kept soaking through their jackets.

They'd been riding for hours, or what felt like it. Without the sun to use as a guide, she had no way to measure the passage of time.

"We should find watches when we next get an opportunity to scavenge," she said. "Manual ones."

"And what do we set them to?" Luis asked. "I never bothered because without the correct time, didn't seem to be any value."

"It doesn't have to be exact," she said. "We'll agree on a time. I just want to be able to tell how long we've been riding, mostly. Maybe make days like these easier to handle."

"It's been about two hours," Luis said.

"Are these hills empty?" Astrid asked.

"I didn't spend time looking," Luis answered. "We can ask at the fort. They keep good patrols. Or they did last time I was around here."

Something rustled the undergrowth. Not wind, the air was still like it didn't have the energy or interest to bother moving the branches above them.

"What kind of wildlife hunts around here?" Tik asked.

"Used to be a few mountain cats, and some goats," Luis said. "Could be wolves. Of course, could be lions and tigers. Lots of zoos let their animals free toward the end."

"It's not their environment," Mellow said. "But a bear? Yes. We need to be careful. They can move fast and take down a horse before you can draw a weapon."

Out of the corner of her eye, Lena saw Astrid bring her crossbow to the front and load a bolt.

Bebop sidestepped and the other horses twitched. "We need to move faster," Lena said.

It wasn't possible to gallop even though Lena could feel Bebop straining at the reins. They rounded the corner and Lena pulled on the reins to stop her horse from barreling into the man standing in the middle of the path.

"Give us all your supplies." Not a man, a boy by the sound of his voice.

"Not going to happen," Astrid yelled before anyone else could speak. "Move aside."

Three others came out of the brush. Lena heard Tik swear and turned to see four more of the young bandits blocking their way back.

"We have nothing you need," Lena said.

A knife flew out from behind a tree. It missed her and buried itself hilt deep in the ground.

"Give us all your supplies," the boy repeated. "Horses, too. And we'll take your weapons. Maybe we let you go then."

How many others hid along the road? Lena was uncertain how to handle the situation and knew that could prove deadly. There was only one way to escape; trample the people and keep moving. But she couldn't choose to simply murder a child who was only trying to survive.

"We give you nothing, and if you don't move, you'll learn what someone who can aim a weapon can do." Astrid was determined to fight her way out. Like she'd been spoiling for this fight since being rescued. Or perhaps building up points for their stay in Fort Revelation, or stories to share with the soldiers.

"More of us," a high voice called from the shadows. "You shoot, we attack. How you going to fight us all?"

Astrid moved Raven forward. He was small and lithe, and now she'd managed to use some patience, she could guide him with her knees. She lifted her crossbow and took aim at the boy who'd addressed them first. "How about we give it a try," she said. "I'll kill this guy first."

"Astrid, wait," Lena said. "You can't just kill anyone standing in our way every time." Perhaps the little gang would hear that and think she had fought more. Think twice about starting something with a professional.

Luis slipped up beside Lena. "Only nine of them." He didn't whisper. He wanted the gang to be aware they'd been caught in a lie.

"Okay, so by the time you get to us, I can take out three," Astrid said as if she were anticipating the deaths. She switched from aiming at the first boy to the people on either side as if to reinforce her threat. "Lena can handle two, has before. That leaves three for the rest of us. Doesn't sound like we're outnumbered."

"This is our territory." The person who'd spoken from the shadows stepped out onto the road. She was slight and looked to be thirteen or so under the grime covering her face.

Somewhere they had a settlement. Was this the entire makeup of the gang, or would they really find themselves outnumbered? And how would they survive when this raid proved unsuccessful?

"You should have asked for a toll," Astrid said. "Now we're going to keep moving. You move out of the way, and we all live to see the sunrise."

No one was getting between Astrid and this fight. Lena looked over to Tik and noticed he was gone. Mellow held Beauty's reins. She gave a tiny nod to Lena. Someone had a plan.

"Where's Jimmy and Lucy?" the girl asked.

Lena looked back to where the road had been blocked by four people. No one was there.

"They got em," the boy said. "Ike and Mimi, too."

Tik stepped out of the trees leading the four young gangsters who were tied together with rope. "Here's your choice. You agree to safe passage and we take these as hostages until we feel safe. Or you fight and I start by putting a knife through their throats."

The girl looked at her companion, then at her captured people. "How long you plan to keep them?"

"Why, you have an appointment?" Tik asked.

Astrid still stood tall in her saddle with her crossbow aimed at the lead boy.

"Need them to hunt," the boy said.

"How far to the edge of your territory?" Lena asked.

"Day's ride," the girl said.

"What stops you attacking us when we leave?" Astrid asked.

"We don't hunt on other people's land." The girl held out her hand. It was grimy and creased with sap. She spat on the palm and held it out again. "You leave our territory by sundown and we're square."

Scott dismounted and spat in his own palm to seal the agreement. "We'll send them back in a couple of hours."

The five standing in their way slipped off the road into the trees.

39

"How far?" Astrid asked. "Before we get there?"

Lena turned away so Luis wouldn't see her smile. The girl asked this question at least five times a day since they'd left the kid gang territory. Luis was doing a poor job of hiding his frustration.

"What did I tell you at breakfast?" he asked.

"A couple of days."

"How long has it been?"

"Maybe half a day?" She hadn't yet realized that he was trying to make her stop asking.

"Do the math," he said and nudged Junior ahead of the group.

Astrid moved next to Lena and shouted, "I thought we might have made up some time."

Lena turned to tell the girl to stop being so impatient and saw the grin. "You really shouldn't tease him like that," she said.

Astrid was shaking with silent laughter. "Too much fun."

Lena decided to stay out of it. Luis was capable of

handling Astrid and after what she'd done to him to escape Virtue. He deserved the satisfaction.

"Can we stop for a few minutes?" Mellow called from the back.

"We'll rest in a couple of hours," Luis answered.

"Not to rest," she said. "There is a stream nearby and I thought I saw some wild strawberry plants growing. We should harvest."

The first day they rode through this part of the mountain, darker and more turned back to nature than the highways, Mellow found some medicinal herbs. Since they'd thrown out all of Siren's in case Nicolette had added unwanted ingredients, they'd been on the lookout for replacements.

The plants and branches didn't take up much room or weigh enough to matter. They would be good trade for any community. Some were rare or hard to harvest, and Mellow was sure that not all communities knew the value. The herbs and her expertise would be worth a night's rest and food. Maybe some travel supplies.

The path was only wide enough for two horses, and in places, narrower than that. Lena wasn't willing to count on the fact that they hadn't seen another traveler for days. "Line up single file. And wait here," she said. "I can see the stream, so Mellow can go by herself."

"I'll help," Siren said. He dismounted and was through the trees before Lena could stop him.

Tik took control of his mount, Scott took Mellow's reins.

"Be quick," Lena said. "We don't know what might be coming to join you for a drink."

"That happens at dawn and dusk," Mellow said.

"And mountain lions don't get thirsty during the day?"

"Okay, we'll shout if we need help." She unhooked the

saddle bag they'd set aside for collecting wet vegetation, lined with paper and drain holes in the bottom, then joined Siren.

"It will be nice to head into a community without a crisis," Lena said.

"We've got two days, yet," Luis said chuckling.

"Are you sure they will let us in?" Scott asked.

Luis shrugged. "I haven't been there for over a year. Things change. But probably they'll see it as Christian charity. Might not be a warm welcome, but do we care?"

"No," Tik said. "At this point, I just want a dry bed and something other than beans or oatmeal for food."

As if answering his call, a light pattering from above and then the first cold drops hit Lena's scalp. "Hurry up," she called out towards the stream.

"I see Camas and Field Mint here too," Mellow answered. "Five minutes."

"We'll be just as wet when we move," Luis said. "What they gather might make the difference."

All the plants would do for food in a pinch, but their medicinal value was the best trade.

"Siren, be careful." Mellow's shout was followed by a splash and a scream.

Lena jumped off Bebop and rushed toward the noise, trusting someone would take the reins.

Mellow was knee deep in the middle of the stream holding Siren's hand as he struggled to stand. She saw Lena and handed her the bag holding their harvest. "Take it or I'll have to let it all go."

"What happened?" Lena put the bag on a large rock and joined Mellow and Siren.

"We were coming back across," Mellow said. "Siren tried to jump from one boulder to another and he slipped. The current is trying to pull him downstream, so I can't let him go."

Siren just moaned and lay in the water.

"How much damage?" Lena asked. She stepped beside Mellow to assess how they would lift the boy if he couldn't manage to stand and walk.

"His arm is broken. The one in the water." Mellow nodded toward where Siren's arm flopped at the wrong angle. "We need to stabilize it, and then he should be able to get up."

"It hurts," Siren said.

"I'm sure it does," Lena said. "Can you sit up at least?"

"No, I can't find leverage."

Maybe the water was too cold for him to use his muscles to lift his body higher.

"I'll find something we can use to immobilize his arm. We have to get him on the path, so we know how bad it is," Lena said to Mellow. Then turning to Siren, she asked, "Did you hit your head?"

"No, and everything else is numb from the cold."

She ran to the bank and picked up the bag of soaking plants. Scott met her halfway to the path. She handed him the basket and told him what to bring. "There's no point in all of us getting drenched in the river. The rain will take care of that soon enough. Can Luis go ahead to see if he can ask someone at this fort place to come help?" Maybe going on his own would make it less time.

She ran back to Mellow and tried to reach under Siren's shoulder to lift him. There was no way they could wrap his arm when it was floating.

"You need to stand. I'll try to hold the break but it's going to hurt."

"Okay." His teeth were chattering.

She nodded to Mellow, who moved to stand in front of Siren and then brace herself. It would be awkward. Mellow could only use his whole arm to pull. She bent it at the elbow and put one hand on his upper arm. Lena gently floated Siren's broken arm to his side and crouched.

"Okay, on three," She mouthed two to Mellow.

"One, two." She pushed, Mellow pulled, and Siren finally got his feet under him.

Scott waited on the bank with a leather belt and one of the spare blankets.

40

Every time Lena tried to move faster, Siren moaned about the pain. She had a faint memory that they could go a while before the break started to heal and would need to be broken again to set it straight, but not how long it was. She hoped for a couple of days.

"If I had my medicines, I could stop the pain," Siren whined.

"If you hadn't disposed of them, you wouldn't be here," Tik said. Storm, his horse, had the smoothest gait, so he continued to share his ride. They'd distributed all the packs, including the ones they'd carried before, between Olive and Angel to lift the strain.

"I wouldn't have a broken arm either," Siren said with a moan.

"Stop complaining," Lena said. "It doesn't stop the pain, and it just irritates us. We're going toward help as fast as your injury allows."

"Should I just grit my teeth and let you gallop?"

She was tempted to say yes, but the boy was in pain and

probably hadn't experienced anything like it in his life. Then she remembered the scars and reassessed her judgment. "Just stop bitching about it. It doesn't help you, and it annoys us."

For a while, they rode in silence. The rain eased up shortly after they left the site of the accident. Trees still dripped from overhead, but that would stop soon. A little dampness wasn't the worst of their problems. Lena worried that they would have to ride in the dark soon. A big risk without anything to light their way.

"Someone's coming," Scott called back from the front. "Two riders."

"Pull to the side and wait," Lena said. "We can't chance that they'll pass without jostling us."

"It's Luis," Scott called back, "and some woman."

As he spoke, Luis came into sight. "Okay, we dismount."

The woman pulled her horse to a halt beside Siren and Tik. "Did you see bone?" Her voice was clipped, like she didn't have time to soften it, or for introductions.

"No," Tik said. "We got it bound within minutes."

"You did a good job." She dismounted and strode to Lena. Her hair was cut short and close to her scalp, a scar on her cheek was a dark line in her black skin. She wore loose camo, which did nothing to hide the lean muscles in her back and shoulders. Maybe in her mid-twenties, but life out here could have aged her faster than time. "Luis says you're the leader here?"

"I'm Lena Custordin. I guess if Luis said so, then I am."

"Beattie. Last name Angler. I'll take the kid through a back door."

"One of us will come with you," Lena said. "He shouldn't be alone."

"Nope. No one but a member of the unit knows about our back gates. I'll give you directions to a closer entrance, but the boy comes with me alone."

Lena looked to Luis for some hint for what she should do.

"There isn't anyone else," he said. "Let her take him."

"Look," Beattie said. "I don't know what Luis told you about Fort Revelation, but things have changed. Commander Greenly will explain. We need to go now, though. If you delay any longer the entrance will be closed for the night. Storm's coming and you'll be out in it."

"If this entrance is so secret, how are you going to stop Siren from seeing it?" Astrid asked. She'd moved up to stand beside Beattie. She stood as tall as she could manage and stared at her like they were about to fight. When had she stopped hinting he should be sent away to becoming so protective of the boy?

"He'd be blindfolded. You've got him bound up well, so I won't have to adjust the splint. If he gets on my ride now, he'll be with the medic in fifteen minutes."

"I'll expect to see him as soon as we get to your Fort Revelation," Astrid said.

She strode back to Raven and mounted as if she'd made the decision. If she was in a combative mood, this fort might be the best place for her. If Beattie was any example, there were a lot of trained soldiers on hand to use up her energy.

"We don't have much choice," Lena said. "Take care of him."

"Right." Beattie mounted her horse and nodded to Siren, who had been unusually quiet through the entire exchange. "Get up here."

"I can't," Siren whined.

She prodded her horse to Storm's side. "Use your good

arm to move across. Don't kick Strider as you move, he'll just let you drop to the ground. I'm thinking you don't want to add to your injuries."

Siren did as he was told. It wasn't graceful, but he managed to slide across to Strider and wrap his unbroken arm around Beattie, keeping the splinted one between them for protection.

"Luis," she ordered him to join her. "The old lightning-hit stump by the ford? Turn up and you'll find a gate maybe an hour straight up."

She didn't wait for him to ask any questions, simply nudged Strider's flank and raced back along the trail. Siren made no noise of pain or complaint.

"We need lessons on how to keep him from moaning all day," Scott said. "How did you find her, Luis?"

"She said the Fort is sending out patrols these days. She was checking on their traps and looking for signs of trouble — probably those kids testing their boundaries. Heard me coming. Came out of the trees, scared the shit out of me."

"Do you know her?" Astrid asked. "Can she be trusted?"

"Met her the last time I was there. She was in jail for speaking up against the reverend running the place. I guess I'd say she can be trusted as long as she thinks we're good people."

"Then I guess that's what we'll be," Mellow said. "Anything else we should be aware of?"

"She wouldn't tell me anything. Loyal to the Greenly guy. Told me to ask him questions when we arrived. Did say they'd be grateful for the herbs, and the knowledge you bring."

"I'm not sure how much knowledge I have, but I'm happy to share." Mellow mounted River. "I guess we should go."

"So, we're all going to be polite," Lena asked looking at Astrid.

"I promise I'll be a good girl," Astrid said. Then she laughed. "I'm not sure I'll get away with anything around Beattie."

41

A metal barrier faced them at the end of a steep trail. Someone had made sure there was no place to camp, and the path forced them to ride single file. A good defensive position if you needed to defend against anything. Lena tried not to worry that the road ahead of them would be filled with bandits.

The gate creaked open and a man in full army gear stood in the center of the opening. He carried what looked like an assault rifle with a long, curved knife in his belt. He had that long stare, like he was some kind of sniper looking for targets in the distance. "You can come in, but don't get comfortable. We don't take in new people."

"Fair enough," Lena said. "We have some trade to do if you are interested. We'll be happy to head out as soon as Siren can travel."

"Your horses can stable with ours. Your belongings can stay in the stable. They'll be safe, I promise. I'll have someone escort you to the command building when you're settled."

He turned to the right and disappeared before anyone could say another word. A second man stepped out and beckoned them in. "Get in quick," he said. "My name's Jones. We don't like the gate open late, so Beattie thinks you're worth a risk. Wait off to the left near the bench. I'll take you to the stables after we have a look at your weapons."

"Are you planning to take them?" Tik asked.

"No, just want to be sure of what you got," Jones said. "Hey, Luis. You know the drill."

The gate creaked shut as Luis brought up the rear. "Jones. Hear things have changed."

Jones asked them to dismount and bring out their weapons. "I'll let Commander Greenly tell you about it."

Lena placed her bow and a handful of bolts on the bench. The others followed suit, except Astrid. Of course she was going to argue.

"Astrid, just do it," Lena said. "We need them to trust us."

"All of my weapons?"

"What do you mean?" They'd been on the road long enough after leaving Liberty that she shouldn't have any secrets. "All?"

Tik moved to stand beside Astrid. "Start bringing them out," he said.

She placed her own bow and bolts on the bench. Then a handful of small knives that didn't have hilts, just a metal projection. Then she reached into her boot and added a skinning knife. One that looked like an army knife came from a sheath in her sleeve and a wire with small metal bars at each end from her pocket.

"Is that all?" Lena asked, trying not to show her shock at the number of knives.

"Yes, unless they want to count the forks and spoons." She held out her arms like she expected to be searched.

"I thought those men stripped you of everything when they took you prisoner," Mellow said.

"I took what I could get my hands on when I left," Astrid said.

Lena couldn't decide if she should be proud or concerned. Astrid had kept her weapons hidden from anyone not involved in training.

"You might want to keep some of your blades in storage," Jones said. "Same as the bows and bolts. No need of them in here."

Lena turned away from the bench without taking her bow and bolts. "Let's get the horses set up and go talk to the man in charge."

Astrid took her garrote and two knives. "Just in case," she said.

Jones stuck close to them the entire time it took to make sure the horses were settled with food and water. He took them to the armory and locked their weapons in a metal box. He handed keys to Lena and Tik. "You can get them any time. I've got a master in case of emergency, but no one else. Not even the commander."

"Our belongings?" Mellow asked. "Where should we put them?"

"You've got the visitor barracks to yourselves, just leave them inside. I don't know about you but I'm ready for dinner and a drink next to the fire."

. . .

JONES POINTED them to what seemed to be a head table in the mess hall. The room was already full of people in camo outfits, all talking and eating and joking around. The camp must hold a couple of hundred people, Lena thought. She'd been trying to work out how big it was based on the fact that Luis's entrance was a day's travel longer than it took them through Beattie's entrance.

Greenly sat alone at their table. He stood and beckoned them over. "Introduce yourself to the room." He banged a hammer on the table to call the attention of the crowd. "These folks are our guests. One of them is in the medic tent. I'll let these tell you about him."

He turned to look at Lena. She hadn't expected this. A military fort would normally be a chain of command structure and people were given information when they needed it. But Fort Revelation was obviously different.

"We're just passing through on our way to the coast," she said. Then she introduced everyone. "The boy with your medics is called Siren. He joined our group a few weeks back. I guess I should say we're exploring the country, what's left of it. Looking for places who want to be part of the future."

"Get back to what you were up to," Greenly said and the noise rose again as people started talking.

"The grub is basic but good," Greenly said as two women put plates in front of them. "Doc tells me your boy can travel in a few days. Won't be comfortable, but if you don't leave soon, you'll have a hard time getting as far as the coast."

"Thanks for your kindness," Mellow said.

"We don't turn away people in need," he said, "but we don't take in anyone. We know our own people. We've dealt with some that don't agree with our ways. Not looking to repeat the experience."

"We have some things to trade," Scott said. "Are you interested?"

"Yes, but we'll talk about that tomorrow."

42

I f this was basic food, Lena wondered what Greenly thought of as special. Roasted potatoes, some kind of vegetable that she didn't recognize, and a perfectly grilled venison steak. The cook had seasoned the meat with herbs that mimicked salt and pepper, both of them in short supply these days.

"Can I check on Siren?" Astrid asked.

"He's resting," Greenly said. "Tomorrow would be better."

"I don't need to talk to him," Astrid said. "I just want to see that he's okay."

"Your boyfriend?" Greenly asked.

"No." Astrid cut into her meat with a level of savagery that made Lena worry about what she was planning.

"We've had some bad experiences with medical help," Lena said. "I think we'd all sleep better after a quick visit."

"I'll ask the medic and he can decide," Greenly said. "I don't care what happened to you before, this is a safe environment. You see him, and then you let go of whatever happened."

"Thank you."

"And I want to check on our weapons," Astrid said. "Maybe keep them with us."

"No visitors go around armed." Greenly poked at his remaining food, not much left but the greens. "You like the fiddleheads?"

"Tastes like asparagus," Scott said. "Hard crop to grow?"

"Needs a lot of space, shade and trees," Greenly said. "Harvest them from the woods. It's better to have some variety. But these are plentiful, so we have them too often."

Lena listened while Greenly and Scott talked about farming. The vegetables did taste like pickled asparagus, so it kind of made sense they were both from a fern. The brine went well with the richness of the meat, and the fat from the roasted potatoes.

Astrid leaned toward Lena and whispered, "I don't like this. We need to be careful."

"It's not the cult," Lena said. "Let's try not to make this hard. We need their help and they've been nothing but welcoming."

"As long as we get out fast," she said. "I want the key to the weapons."

Lena glanced over to where Greenly was still talking about farming with Scott. No one in the hall was paying much attention to the head table, so maybe Astrid's paranoia was going unnoticed.

"I don't like any of this, Astrid. But we can't expect to be invited to join any community. You wanted training, and this is the perfect place for it. Even a couple of days with these military types will help. Even more now, because they can't rely on assault rifles, so they've honed other skills."

Astrid pulled back from Lena, a frown on her face. Before Lena could tell her not to make things worse, she said, "I didn't think of that. They can't train me without weapons, right?"

Trust the girl to find a way to achieve everything she wanted.

"Commander Greenly," Astrid said in that sweet tone she used when she wanted something, "do you think I can train with your soldiers while we're here?"

"Hand to hand, sure," he said.

"I was thinking more about knives," she said. "You know, throwing and stuff."

"You aren't getting your blades back until you leave," he said.

"You don't trust me?"

"Let's say I've worked with a lot of eager youngsters. You'll need to prove what you can be trusted with."

"I'm not a kid," Astrid said.

Lena looked down at her plate to hide her smile.

"You are," Greenly said. "Even for these days, you have no experience in real battle. It's different from one-on-one and it's not something you can learn over a few days."

"So, we stay longer," she said.

"No. You go when the medic says your boy is ready to travel."

"But."

Greenly held up his hand to stop her from continuing. "No buts, young lady. Our rules, not yours and we don't negotiate. Learned that lesson early on." He turned and looked over the other tables. He pointed at a group of diners. "Angler, up here." He didn't raise his voice, but Beattie stood and joined them.

"What do you need?" she asked.

"This girl is determined to get her own way. You take her. Make sure she learns what real fighting is about."

"Yes, sir." Beattie looked at Astrid, then at her plate. "Good, you finished your meal. Join us."

Astrid's eyes lit up. "For real?"

"We have our orders. You'll rejoin your people for sleep, but you stick with me until time comes for you to go." Beattie didn't wait for Astrid to respond. She turned and rejoined her group.

"You got what you asked for," Lena said. "Try not to get into too much trouble."

Astrid took her plate and added it to the pile waiting to be washed. She didn't quite run to the table, but it was clear she didn't want to waste a moment.

"Thanks," Lena said. "She's been through some awful experiences. It will be good for her to learn from people who are adept at fighting."

"We've all lived through shit," Greenly said. "Everyone lost people. Either in the plague or just from surviving since."

"Hard to argue with that," Lena said. "I'd love to talk about trade and connections."

Greenly nodded and then drained his mug. "Tomorrow at dinner. We all have work to do, and you'll get a taste of what we're about." He rose and left them.

"I can't get a read on him," Tik said. "Luis, what do you know about this place?"

Luis glanced around the room before answering. "It's changed since I was last here, like I said. But, yes, I'm not sure if it's for better or worse."

"He agreed we could check on Siren," Mellow said. "After that, I need sleep."

"We should all rest," Lena said. "We'll be up early."

43

Lena woke with a jerk at the sound of a bugle. This was taking the army thing too far. She joined the others in rolling out of bed and checking the windows. The sun was barely showing.

Astrid ran to the bathroom and slammed the door.

"She's heading to the training ground after breakfast," Mellow said. "I guess she isn't going to eat with us and delay her start."

Five minutes later she was running out the door. "See ya later."

Despite her demands at dinner, Astrid had barely looked in on Siren. The boy was still in pain, but his arm was encased in plaster, and the medic said he'd survive.

"Are we splitting up today?" Tik asked. "Take in as much as we can and then share?"

"I guess that will be up to the commander," Lena said.

"I think we need to have a plan," Luis said. "I'll be looking for what's changed. These were good people, but more on the far-right religious side of the survivalist life. I didn't see any of the old leaders. Be nice to know what happened to them."

"If we have a chance to split up," Mellow said, "I'll check out the medic. That's where I can get the most information. And I can figure out what they need. Maybe help with the negotiations."

"Farming," Scott said. "This is very different from our climate, but I'm sure I'll learn something."

"Astrid will be all over the defensive aspect," Tik said. "I'll check out their animal management, maybe learn how they make arrows and bolts while I'm at it. Stuff we learned in Beta will come in handy for them."

Lena hoped Greenly would let them wander. All of the information would be valuable, and harder to find if he assigned them a guide like they were tourists. "I'll talk to people."

At breakfast, Greenly agreed to let them see whatever they chose, but not to wander alone. Each of them had a guide to answer questions and make sure they didn't get lost or in the way, according to the commander.

"I don't have any particular interest," Lena said when she was alone with Greenly.

"Then we'll have Lori give you the ten-cent tour," he said beckoning a woman from the back of the room. "You're the leader, right? Of your home community?"

She hated the idea of being in charge, but everyone treated her like she was the boss. "Reluctantly, yes."

"It's hard, right?"

The woman joined them. In her fifties and as fit as any of the younger soldiers, she snapped to attention and waited for orders.

"Lori, take Lena around and show her how we manage."

"The defenses?" Lori asked.

"Let's keep some things off limits. I don't want to have to make too many changes after they leave," he said. "Treat her like a visiting dignitary. She might have some ideas about how to make things work a little better, or pick up a few ideas." He turned to Lena. "I'm heading out on patrol. I'll see you at dinner. We'll have a better idea of how your young man is healing. Make some trade plans."

He didn't wait for her to answer.

LORI TOOK HIS ORDERS LITERALLY. Lena followed her around the compound all day. Not just the part they'd seen, but on horseback to the other end of the compound and back. The fencing surrounding them changed with the environment. Solid metal walls gave way to razor wire. At one point, the edge of the community hit the top of a cliff with no barrier. Two guard huts sat overlooking the edge.

"We keep an eye out, but anyone climbing up here is going to be in poor shape for fighting." Lori checked the sun's position. "We'll grab some lunch and then head back. Give you time to talk to your people. Share what you learned today."

Lena opened her mouth to deny they'd been gathering information and then closed it. It was no secret, so why pretend? "We've picked up a lot of information along the way," she said. "We like to spread the new ways people find to do more than just scratch out an existence."

Lori led Lena to a small clearing just beyond the cliff. They sat and she brought out a mess bag and handed Lena a sandwich and a jar of pickled carrots.

"You come from back east, right? A farm?"

"Near what used to be Manitoba," Lena said. "A few

local towns joined us. We all contribute something to make everyone's life better."

"Nice," Lori said.

"Luis tells us the fort has changed in the last year or so," Lena said.

"The commander will tell you everything he wants you to hear," Lori said. "You want to see anything else?"

"I think your suggestion of going back to the barracks will be fine." Lena had seen enough of their fortifications to wonder who would be attacking. She didn't feel safe out here on the edges, regardless of the guards and fences.

44

Dinner was a bowl of hearty venison stew with peas and potatoes. And a side of pickled mushrooms. The fort must be short on other curing options.

"Good day?" Greenly asked as he joined her. Other than Astrid, who was sitting with Beattie at a table with other soldiers, and Siren who was still in the care of the medic, her group was at the same head table.

"I think so," Lena said. "Is it a good time to talk about trade and maybe another idea?"

"We need medicines, which I don't think you have. But Mellow here knows about plants, and she's told the medic where to look for some things that will help. Your man Scott gave our gardeners a few ideas, and Tik gave the armorers the plans for those bolts you brought. Not sure we'll find enough metal, but we'll see."

So, negotiation seemed redundant because everything they had to offer was already handed over. "We could use a few things," Lena said.

Greenly barked out a laugh. "We weren't planning on

stiffing you. We have crates of MREs. Easy to pack enough to last you a month. Anything else?"

The military rations were designed to last forever and be edible even without water or a fire. "That's more than I expected," Lena said.

"We think your boy should have a few more days," Greenly said. "You can work for your board."

"Do you get many visitors," Lena asked as the meal wound down. "Your defenses are impressive."

"We're pretty hidden," Greenly said. "Had some trouble a while back, so we all agreed to be prepared. It's not like we have much else to do these days. I don't like the idea of having all these trained fighters sitting idle."

"What about the future?" Lena asked. "I'm trying to build some kind of alliance across the country. Nothing like the old days, but maybe just a few agreed-upon rules so it's safe to travel. Shared services."

"You think we're ready for that?"

"It worked at home," Scott said. "Helped us win a fight to hang onto our farm."

"So, you had a need," Greenly said. "Yeah, that is how it works. People come together to solve a problem. To get them to do it without the threat is a big project."

Lena understood. She was no stranger to the idea people needed a burning platform to change, but there must be something she could do now. "If we all stay separate, eventually it will be too hard to join up, and the threat might win because we won't unite."

"I hear you. Look, this place is a democracy. It is now, anyway. I'll put it to a vote. If the majority want to join up with your idea, we'll do it."

"Why the change?" Luis asked. "Last time I was here,

you were run by the people who set up the place. Church of the Pure."

"They got a little too focused on our souls," Greenly said. "We convinced them to head out. Think they went south."

It didn't sound like he wanted to get into the details.

"What happens if the vote goes the other way?" Mellow asked.

"I think we need to know what's going on out beyond our fences," Greenly said. "I'll send someone along with you. They'll come back and report. That work?"

Another mouth to feed? At least they would be able to fight and train Astrid. So far, Siren had done little more than help set up and take down their camp. And Astrid had just been a bundle of potential.

Maybe they would be able to convince Greenly that the world would be better if it was more united. "Who?" she asked.

"Beattie. She's been taking on more than her share of patrols. I think she's getting a bit of camp fever."

45

The next day, Greenly assigned everyone tasks pretty much following what each had researched the day before. Lena was sent over to the stores to pick out what they would take when they left. MREs, some canteens, and an extra set of clothes for each of them. She didn't want to take advantage of his generosity. She also didn't want anything that would weigh them down. Beattie said she would arrange her own supplies before she took Astrid for a session with the soldiers.

When Greenly called her to the table, Beattie had agreed to join the group. Not just agreed; she'd been eager to come. The man knew his people well.

Now, just before lunch, Lena watched Astrid train. The area was fenced off. Targets lined the back, facing the woods, and bulky sacks hung from poles, used for hand-to-hand combat training.

Astrid was facing off with Beattie. They'd been training with staves all morning, both were sweating, but Astrid was also dirty. She'd taken a lot of falls in the short time Lena stood at the training ground. There was no anger or pouting when it happened; she got up and kept trying.

"She's come a long way," Luis said. He'd come up to stand beside Lena without her noticing.

"A good trainer. We've got skills, but none of us have ever done more than teach a few locals to fight." It had been more than that. The battle with Newton Cole's men had been vicious and took lives. But Lena was under no illusions about the outcome if they'd faced actual soldiers, not just bullies.

"We need to leave in the next day or so," Luis said. "You think Siren will be ready?"

"Are you suggesting we leave him here?"

"Greenly won't let us. I hinted at it, and he turned the idea down." Luis watched the two women as he spoke. "That Beattie will be a good addition."

"We can't keep adding people," Lena said. "I didn't plan on leading every community's exploration campaign."

"It might be the way you get your vision in place," Luis said. "You're creating a relationship with every person."

"That's great. You think Jacob and the rest of Virtue will listen to Astrid if she tells them how good my idea is? Or Nicolette?"

"You've got a point, but I think this place will listen to Beattie."

"That's not a good return, one out of three people will help?"

"So, you give up?"

Lena wondered if that was an option. She could let someone else join the communities into a larger unit. It would take years to do, maybe longer than she was willing to travel. "Not give up," she said. "Maybe I'm jumping over some steps. Maybe what I'm doing is the first. Not getting people to agree, but sparking the idea? Planting the seed for someone else to harvest."

"Never built a country before, but that sounds like sense," Luis said.

"What about you?" Lena asked. He was so much a part of her group that she sometimes forgot that he'd joined them on the trail. "Are you going to stick with us?"

Luis smiled, something rare for him. "I won't disappear on you, Lena. I'm not saying I'm in for the whole journey, but I'll let you know before I go, if I leave. I haven't been to your home area, so maybe I'll stay to visit this farm."

"Good." Lena rolled her shoulders to stretch out the tension she felt. "I should check on Siren. See for myself how much more time we need to spend here."

"He's helping out with light duties," Luis said. "I just came from there. Medic would like to keep him for a few more days but said he could leave tomorrow. No galloping and no heavy duties."

"Not that much different from the entire time he's been with us," Lena said with a chuckle. "Let's find out if our two warriors are ready for a break. I'd like to learn a bit about Beattie before we hit the road with her."

AT DINNER THAT NIGHT, the head table consisted of Greenly, Luis, and Lena. The others ate with the people they'd worked with.

"Vote is done," Greenly said.

"I didn't see anything about it," Lena said. "Remember how votes happened before? Thank god it's changed."

"It's easier now because we don't have so much game-playing. I send a rider out to collect the votes from the guards on the perimeter. The rest just dropped off theirs during the day."

"And?" Lena didn't expect a yes, but any information might be useful as they passed other places on their journey.

"Sorry, no one is ready to agree to anything," Greenly said.

"Okay, thanks for trying. We'll be out of your way tomorrow."

"It's not all bad news," Greenly said. "The vote isn't yes or no. We found out early on that it was an opportunity for everyone to contribute ideas. Faster than calling a meeting. And mostly, people do have some other ideas."

"Doesn't getting ideas slow everything down?" Luis asked. "You need to get clarification on suggestions, or talk it out somehow?"

"Sometimes. When people vote, they say yes or no. Or they can drop a suggestion, or they can demand a town hall. Never been a problem."

"So, you got suggestions," Lena said. "What do you need from us?"

"Nothing. The vote was no by a narrow margin, but almost everyone said they needed more information. They couldn't decide based on what we know about the world. I admit we stick here more than we probably should."

So not a complete turn down. "Are you going to send out scouting parties?" Lena asked.

"Already have," Greenly said. "Beattie. She'll report back at some point. We're in no hurry. She'll cut out when she thinks she has something to tell us."

46

"This feels like a vacation," Scott said.

They'd seen a sign to a small community near a lake just after stopping for lunch. Luis said it had been abandoned the last time he came through, so Lena sent Beattie and Astrid ahead to check it out while the others approached more slowly.

Nothing had changed. They'd taken an old motel as their camp. The rooms were closed off, so stale and mildew smelling, but secure.

Lena and Scott had set up on the deck of the old swimming pool. It was long emptied of water and filled with dried leaves and other detritus from years of winter storms. A rustle in the far corner indicated they weren't the only residents. But it was better than sleeping bags on a slight widening of the road. The pool faced west and displayed the mountains between them and their destination as a dark point with a dusting of white at the tops.

"If I close my eyes," she said, "and don't breathe too deeply, sure. It does feel good to be making progress and not starving."

"I wanted to say something while we're alone," Scott said.

"Good or bad?" Lena asked. They didn't keep secrets from Mellow or Tik, so it wasn't likely to be the former.

"I don't know if it's either. And I meant, alone from strangers." He shuffled a little closer and put his arm around her. "It's about them. There's four new people with us."

"You're worried we'll be outnumbered soon?" Lena hadn't given it that kind of thought. But if it came down to a disagreement, or even a difficult decision, their control could easily slip. Astrid was bound to side with Beattie, but Siren and Luis might not. "If we have to split up, it can just be the four of us again."

"True, but I was thinking more about when we go back. Yes, it's likely to be a year from now, and we'll know them better, or they'll be long gone. I don't want to take anyone back to the farm. Not yet."

She thought about the idea of bringing Luis and Astrid back to join her family at the farm. "Beattie and Siren will return to their communities, right?"

"Maybe. Beattie, I think yes. Siren, I'm not sure if he's feeling like he'd be welcome now his arm isn't perfect, the way Nicolette likes her followers."

"Do we need to decide now?" Lena asked. Sitting in the dimming light with the man she'd come to love was a rare experience on the road. "I kind of like just being here with you right now."

He pulled her in for a kiss and then held her at arm's length to watch her reaction. "Not right now. I wanted you to know how I felt. I'll talk to Tik and Mellow over the next couple of days."

"What if they want to stay somewhere?" Lena asked.

"We've been thinking about who wants to join us, not about anyone leaving."

"It's a different problem. I don't see it happening, but I was on the road a long time before we met. People change."

She nodded and leaned back into his shoulder. "You aren't the only one who's been thinking," she said. "I'm wondering if this is all worthwhile. No one is interested in forming a union. Maybe we should just head home in the spring rather than looping south."

"Did you really expect people to jump at a chance to unite?" he asked.

"When you put it that way, I sound like an idiot." She chuckled. "Maybe I am. I started this because I thought there would be a better way than just waiting for the next threat to my home. I might just be inviting that threat by talking to other leaders."

"You are not an idiot. This idea is solid. History proves out that we all do better when we work together. Humans have made alliances since day one."

"And war," she said.

"Yes, but the trend has been toward cooperation. Look, you are just trying to do too much all at once." He hugged her shoulders close.

"It's not the first time I've heard that or thought it."

The sun dipped behind the mountains they'd be crossing tomorrow, hiding the outlines. The road wouldn't go as high as the white line of new snow before they found a way down, but soon the line would drop lower and reach the road, making it impassable. This camp might be better than the roadside, but it would not do for the entire winter.

Someone lit a fire in a pit just behind them. In moments, Lena heard the sizzle of food in a pan, and the aroma of grilling fish reached her. The MREs they'd eaten at lunch were filling, and tastier than bean soup, but any fresh food was welcome.

"It's like that," Scott said, nodding his head to point to the fire. "Maybe you're just lighting the furnace. You've left an idea behind every time you've talked to someone, even in Virtue. Some of those ideas will flourish, some will die out."

Lena pushed herself up to join the others around the campfire. "So, we keep to the original plan? Winter on the coast, then home through the south. Spark a few more furnaces?"

"Yes. At least we'll go home with knowledge, and a few friends."

47

The weather turned on them the next day. The rain brought cold along with the weight of wet clothes. Lena worried about when it would turn to snow. They needed to move faster to make Seattle early enough to settle in for the winter.

"The food won't last," Beattie said as she urged her horse next to Bebop. "We need to double ration in this weather. The meals were designed for warmer times, not enough fat in each one to keep us going. The cold is burning more calories."

"I guess it was too much to expect we wouldn't have supply problems," Lena said. "I don't know what we can trap or hunt in this weather."

"It's a blessing in a way," Beattie said. "The main predators won't be out as much, but they might be hungry enough to try for our food. The smaller game is still there, but stopping to trap them will delay us more than benefit us."

It was never going to end, Lena thought. A new challenge always cropped up, and without cars or planes, or trains, they moved too slowly to avoid winter on the road. "Do you have a suggestion? Or is this just a bitch session?"

Beattie grinned at her. "I know we said we were sticking to your plan, but I think we should head south sooner rather than later. There's an opportunity to enter the highway in a few miles and get below this elevation pretty fast."

"The road doesn't feel safe," Lena said, remembering the creepy sensation of being observed when they first set out. "And the weather won't be much better lower."

"It's not safe up here," Beattie said. "If we use the highway, and we're lower down, sure it will still be cold, but the snow will come later. There will be more shelters and more communities to check out, maybe trade with for supplies."

Lena turned to look back on the group behind them. She was in the lead today, Beattie at her side, Astrid almost riding nose to tail with the soldier. Luis, in the rear with the packhorse. Scott, Tik, and Mellow spread out with Siren in the middle. They all looked dejected. Maybe it was because of the rain; they all kept their heads down to avoid the worst of it. Maybe they were wondering if the trip was worth it. Last night, inside the motel, with the fire pit glowing, everyone had been maybe not enthusiastic, but determined to continue. Would the answer be the same if she asked now?

"We can talk when we break for lunch," Lena said. "It's tempting, but do we have any information about the road ahead? We can't keep going until we hit good weather. It feels like we're handing control over to nature."

"Portland?" Beattie asked.

Lena shrugged, not as much of a change as she feared. "Pretty much the same idea as Seattle, but more south."

She couldn't muster any argument either way. The original plan had been the coast, and Seattle seemed more attainable when they sat around the kitchen table. The only thing she was sure of was that they couldn't keep changing the destination. Or maybe that was wishful thinking.

"How high are we?" she asked, not really expecting a usable answer.

"We're getting close to the edge of my range," Beattie admitted. "The snow line is usually a bit higher at this time of year, so I guess it's going to hit here fast, maybe two days."

"And we aren't going downhill all the time, right?" Lena estimated that over those two days, they would ride up to meet the snow before they started the real descent. "Okay, but everyone gets to decide. Maybe Luis has some information about the route that will help."

LUNCH WAS EATEN STANDING beside the horses because there was no dry spot. The animals needed to rest and eat as much as the humans. Lena handed two MREs to each person.

"You should eat the main meals now," Beattie said. "The rest just eat as we ride."

Lena waited until they'd finished the food before raising Beattie's idea. "So, we need to decide now," she said. "The turnoff is not that far. Do we continue in the mountains, where the main threat is nature, or head on the highway where we have no idea what the threat is?"

"It wasn't too bad the last time I came through," Luis said. "Mostly farmers here. The larger places had gangs, but no one gave me any trouble."

"Gangs change," Tik said. "They need resources, and victims, so it may be more dangerous. But if we're careful, we should be okay."

"Will it be faster? Or smoother?" Siren asked. "I could take more speed if the road wasn't so rough."

"I'm in," Scott said. "Seattle was just a place, no reason we have to stick with it."

Astrid, as usual over the last day or two, agreed with Beattie. Mellow took a look around as if the trees would answer her questions.

"There's nothing worth gleaning here," she said. "I mean, some things, but it will be difficult to scavenge. I say we go south. But we stick to it unless something bad happens. We can't really afford to keep changing our plans."

"Okay," Lena said. "Fingers crossed; we'll get out of the rain too. Luis, any idea how long it will take to ride to the city proper?"

"You planning to go right into the city center? Might be better to check out a suburb first."

Lena visited Portland in the time before the plagues. The city was small, but she knew residential areas dotted the edges. "How long to get close enough to figure that out?"

"Week and a half, maybe two? Depends on how fast we can move." He paused for a moment as if he was dredging up a memory. "I didn't go in last time I was near. Not sure if it's safe."

The supplies would run out before they got to the city. A problem for the future, Lena thought. "We'll get on the road then. Stop at the first dry place to rest. Leave before dawn and travel as long as we can each day. If we see signs of communities, we can visit them later, maybe on the way back. If we hit trouble, we'll deal with it. At least we have a couple of trained fighters with us this time."

48

L ena stared out at the bridge leading to Portland. The city looked intact, not that she expected it to be in ruins, but no sign of fighting or recent trouble seemed reassuring. The trip here had been a grind. After the first few days, they'd stopped checking out the small towns just off the highway. It took time, and every single community was abandoned. Perhaps the people had migrated toward the city. Unlike the bigger places, this one had lots of green space for farming, and was on the river for fishing. Providing for a large population would be, if not easy, not too hard. Or maybe everyone had moved south for gentler weather.

"We need to go in before dark," Beattie said. "We need to see what we're doing, find a place to hole up while we get oriented, and find food."

The MREs had lasted until two days ago. They'd left the horses yesterday in a barn. Lots of food, water, and room until they decided it was safe to bring them into the city. The group carried their remaining supplies in backpacks.

"A house will probably be good," Lena said. "On the

outskirts. Unless everyone came here, some should still be vacant and livable."

"We won't know until we go in," Beattie said. "What do you think?"

It was mid-morning. Lena hated the idea of being exposed on the bridge as they approached. It reminded her of their escape from New Surrey. "Does Luis have an opinion?"

"I don't know this place," he said as he joined them. "From here it could be mayhem. We should wait until dark to cross the bridge. Huddle down where we can until morning."

There was camp space where they stood. Scott and Mellow were exploring the area for anything they could forage. Astrid and Tik were looking for a higher perch to look into the buildings. Siren sat under a tree cradling his arm as though it hurt. It probably did, but without pain killers he'd have to endure it.

"Let's get everyone's report," Lena said. "We could go in early, cross the bridge before dawn, then we can see how good or bad it is right away."

"We need to be off the road if we're planning to hang out here," Beattie said. "I can't be sure if it's safe over the other side of the bridge, but I plan on acting like it isn't."

To be so close to the end of the journey was frustrating. They were looking at the only option for winter and now they were afraid to take the final step. There were other towns, both south and west of Portland, but none came with a guarantee of safety. "We'll talk," Lena said. "I don't think we can wait long. Unless Scott and Mellow find something, we'll be starving soon. We'll have no energy to fight if we have to."

"An hour isn't going to make a difference," Luis said.

"We'll get under the trees and talk. That city is only an hour's walk away. You've crossed the entire continent, no need to rush in here."

Tik and Astrid were the first to return. "We should have looked for binoculars or something," Astrid said. "It's too far to be sure what we're seeing."

"I don't know what we expected," Tik said. "It's been a long time, maybe any trouble is over. Or maybe the gangs won here, like they did in other places. We just have to go in blind."

Mellow joined them a moment later. "Not much," she said. "Scott is bringing a few bits, but I don't think it's dry enough for a fire. Most of this will need cooking to make it edible."

We don't have any choices left, Lena thought. Too many things we should have done to prepare.

She shared their discussion when Scott returned, dirty with mud from digging up some tubers that he shoved in a bag.

"So, we go in now and risk being caught if there's trouble. Or we rest here and try to cross before dawn." Astrid looked around at the dripping trees and then the sky. "I vote we go now and find somewhere dry to sleep. We've been hungry before."

"Commander Greenly would have us split up," Beattie said. "Spread the risk. We can see enough to pick a rendezvous point. We go in two groups. Siren will need help, so me, Tik, Scott go first and make sure the meeting point is safe. We can all fight if we need to, and we can leave someone to meet you if we move on. Astrid comes with the second group. Siren should be fine."

"I am not a child," Siren said. "I can protect myself."

It was the first time in days that he'd done anything but moan about pain.

"You can't fight with that arm. Maybe in a few days, but not yet." Lena dug in her pack to find a scarf. She bound Siren's arm tighter to his body, ignoring his intake of breath like it hurt. "Anyone disagree with Beattie's plan?"

She expected Astrid to complain about being separated, but the girl didn't speak. Perhaps being assigned as their fighter made it acceptable. They shifted subtly into the two groups.

"Where are we going to meet?" Mellow asked.

"There's a big sign on a building just past the bridge," Tik said. "Big deer jumping and it says Portland Oregon, maybe something else underneath. Should be easy to find."

"Then we go," Beattie said. "You come after we're out of sight, should be about half an hour when we are past the bridge peak."

"Be careful," Lena said.

49

Lena let Luis take the lead and kept close to Siren. She didn't trust the boy to keep quiet if something bumped him. Luis took them across slowly, looking carefully at each abandoned car or broken concrete barrier. Scott had left a disarmed trap for them at the entrance to the bridge.

This mess wasn't the result of a mass exodus; it was a carefully placed obstacle course, each car forcing them through a route that slowed them down. Keeping people out or slowing them down enough to give whoever ran the city time to set up a defense.

She hoped it was from the beginning, and the residents of Portland were less combative than the bridge indicated.

Luis had found three more trip wires. None were attached to anything more dangerous than a simple collapse of a stack of noisy debris; not set to kill, just warn. But that might be because they didn't have access to explosives.

"Good thing we didn't try in the dark," Astrid whispered. "I'll go join Luis. We can move faster if two of us check for traps."

Lena thought back to the wild card Astrid was before their stop at Fort Revelation. She nodded and held Siren back when he tried to join the girl.

"We need you to get across without doing more damage," she said. "Stick between me and Mellow."

"Sorry I'm such a burden," he said with a sigh.

Still acting the martyr.

"Just don't make it worse," Lena said. "We're almost at the peak of the bridge. We'll see the building in a few minutes." The bridge didn't rise very much in the center, more an extension of the highway than a graceful arc across a river. But it rose enough to obscure the view of the city.

BY THE TIME they were across, the sun was starting to drop. It would be a long time before dark, but exploring the city would need to wait. Lena kept the group together as Luis led them toward the brick building that sat beside what was an open-air market.

There were no vendors or customers, or loiterers. Perhaps commerce was restricted to only certain days, because Lena saw signs that it wasn't abandoned. Cleared of most debris, tables and kiosks set up, some with roll shutters secured. If the city ran to gangs, there must be some kind of peace agreement for exchange of supplies. If it was a more peaceful community, it was likely on a schedule that allowed farmers and other producers to gather merchandise between sales days.

The area was silent, something that gave Lena more worry than reassurance. The feeling of someone taking aim at her had her glancing up to the rooftops every few steps.

"Scott," Luis said and tipped his head toward the side of the building.

He was leaning through a doorway and beckoning them. Luis didn't let them speed up. Running could attract the attention they were hoping to avoid.

"It's clear and we have a place to rest," Scott said as they crossed the threshold. "There's nothing here to support us, or any space we can make safe, so we can't stay."

"Did you notice anything suspicious?" Astrid asked. "Does Beattie think we are safe to explore?"

"Not all of us," Beattie said as she stepped from a doorway. "In here. I think it's best if we only send a few people to scout. I don't like this atmosphere of abandonment when it's obvious people live and trade here."

So not just me, Lena thought.

"Siren stays," Mellow said. "He doesn't have the stamina to scout. You, Astrid, Tik, maybe Scott? The rest of us will stay here. Explore the building to find out if there are any bits and pieces we can use."

Mellow was becoming the leader Lena hoped for. Someone to pass the farm to when she got too tired to run it. Someone who could help the next generation find their way.

"We split into two groups," Beattie said. "I'll take Astrid. Be back by the time the sun hits the hills. Gives us time to move before full dark."

No one waited for any more discussion. Lena found herself alone with Siren, Mellow, and Luis. The room was bare of furniture, and the brick walls didn't have insulation; it would be damp and cold in bad weather. Today the skies had cleared, but they needed more protection than they had by tomorrow. This area wasn't known as the 'wet coast' for fun. Rain was coming and might be settling in for months.

"How is he?" she asked Mellow, who was checking Siren's arm.

"The break is knitting," she said. Lena watched her place a hand above and below the fracture and move them. It made her queasy, but this time the arm remained firm. "As long as he doesn't bang it again, he'll be fine."

"Does that mean I don't need to be wrapped up like a baby?" Siren sounded relieved.

"We'll make a splint for a few days, but no, you don't need that much protection, and you'll be able to work when we're settled. I'm glad we cut the cast off."

Luis moved to the open door. "I'll check the building for something you can use as a splint and look for any potential problems."

"Don't be too long," Lena said. "I'll come looking for you if I start worrying."

"I thought you were smarter than that," he said. "We're already too split up for my comfort. I'll be fast. If I see anything promising, I'll come back and tell you."

LUIS RETURNED before the scouting parties. He carried a couple of slats from a broken pallet and a half-filled burlap sack. "Found some apples," he said, holding out the sack. "Mostly shriveled, but they should be edible. I tossed the moldy ones."

Mellow tied a scarf around Siren's arm to hold the splint before checking the fruit. "Yeah, it will hold us for a while."

Footsteps sounded outside, like someone was creeping toward them. Lena pulled out her knife, Luis did the same. Mellow stood between the door and Siren, with one of the remaining slats in her hands.

"It's us," Beattie said. "Sorry, we should have picked a signal before we went."

Both teams were back at the same time.

"Found a house that will work only a few blocks away," Tik said. "The whole street is empty, but there's a garden in back with some food still growing."

"Anything else?" Lena asked. "Is it safe? Are we settling for something rather than leaving?"

"Let's get to the place before we talk about safety," Tik said.

50

The house was updated, and Lena figured it was only recently abandoned. No evidence of vermin taking over, no debris piled in the corner, and all the windows and doors were intact.

"Are you sure this place is available?" Mellow asked as they entered the living space.

"As sure as we can be," Beattie said. "No one in any of the other houses on the street, and the garden hasn't been tended to in a while."

"If anyone comes, we can deal with it," Astrid said. "We need shelter, and we're staying here for months, so don't worry."

"If someone comes," Beattie said before anyone else could react, "we will talk to them, find a way to avoid a fight and if we have to, we'll move along. I'm not settling here for a winter-long battle."

Astrid shrugged but Lena could see the hurt in her expression at the gentle rebuke. Beattie was right; if they were going to survive the winter, they couldn't start a fight. "Tomorrow we'll do more searching," Lena said. "Tonight, we need to rest, and eat whatever we can find in the garden that doesn't need cooking."

THE NIGHT PASSED WITHOUT INTERRUPTION. Shortly after they'd harvested the last of the carrots and radishes, the rain started. At first it was a gentle fall, then it grew into a downpour that battered the windows and exposed a couple of leaks in the roof.

No supplies were left in the house, and their only food was dried beans or oatmeal, both uncooked. The living room had a fireplace, but when Scott tested it by lighting a rolled-up magazine, the smoke flowed back into the room. The flue was stuck, or the chimney blocked. They would need to find a new way to heat the home and cook whatever they found while scavenging.

They'd each sat watch for a few hours and slept for the rest. It seemed that the fatigue from their last push to reach the city, along with the sound of rain, helped them to find sleep.

Now, it was morning, and Lena was staring out of the window at the neighborhood. The house was tucked close to the highway. A narrow sidewalk and street sat between their front door and the safety fence along the main road. It would have been a noisy place in the time before.

"Found a shed out back," Tik said as he joined her. "We can create a fire pit inside, cut a hole in the roof for ventilation. We just need to find something to cook."

"Good. We still need a way to heat this place, but that can wait a bit."

"Beattie says we should scavenge together," Tik said. "She doesn't want anyone getting lost. We stick as a group until we know a lot more about where we live."

"You feel like arguing with her?"

"Astrid would have my guts," he said with a laugh. "But why would we ignore her? She has the skills to keep us safe."

"True. We need a list. Food, always food, but we need other things, too. Extra sleeping bags. Flashlights, batteries. Maybe something to help us clear up the problem with the fireplace. Clothes."

"We don't have to get it all today," Tik said. "Food and scouting are the priorities."

Lena nodded. She understood logically that they had a long time to settle in, but so long on the road, moving every day more or less, and the thought of the long winter months had her feeling antsy about waiting.

"THESE HOUSES ARE ALL EMPTY," Scott said. "Should we take over a couple more? Or maybe check to see which is the best option?"

The group had moved around the neighborhood entering and checking each house in turn. There were benefits to each one, including an operating fireplace in three of them. "I don't like the idea of us setting up separate residences. If something happens, we should be together." Lena glanced around the last house. "I'm kind of sorry the rain stopped. We need to find out if any of the roofs are more solid."

"Time for that," Beattie said. "I made note of where we might want to move. We should make that decision right away. But I found stores a block away. We need to check those out and then go back for any discussion."

"What stores?"

Beattie beckoned the others to join them. "Whole Foods,

some supply stores. I'm not expecting full shelves, but the cities were hit hardest, right? Lots of people dead real fast. The survivors wouldn't be able to take everything."

"If there's a hardware store, we might find a heater with some fuel," Tik said. "The rain will be back soon. We should be back home within a couple of hours to avoid a soaking."

THE STREET WAS LINED with stores. Whole Foods and an Asian market faced each other. A hipster hardware store and a drug store completed one side of the street, an art supply and a cafe the other.

"We can split up now," Astrid said, glancing at Beattie as if for permission.

"Focus on food," Tik reminded them. "I'll see if I can find anything useful in the hardware store."

"I'll check the drug store," Mellow said. "Astrid should come with me."

"I'll stay out here," Beattie said. "Luis with me. We'll signal if trouble is coming. Be fast and be careful."

The stores had been scavenged, but not completely. They found cans of soup, some pasta in sauce, and dry goods. The hardware place gave them heaters, a camp stove, fuel for both, and a long-handled brush that Tik said might help clear a chimney. Lena was optimistic that they could survive even if there was no community here to join.

On the way back to the house with their loot, Lena heard evidence that they were not alone. A clatter of shots — someone had saved bullets — a scream came from the distance.

"We'll need to be careful," she whispered. "Stay close to the house and keep watch."

51

"I don't like this," Tik said. "They have guns, and we can't hide from them for long. They probably know we took things from the stores. We should go."

They were sitting in the living room with the heater on and the camp stove in the kitchen ready to make dinner. Lena understood Tik's fear. She felt it herself, and she wasn't an ex-gang member. Tik must be terrified of being dragged back in. It wouldn't happen; he had people to fight for him this time. But fear didn't listen to reason.

"We're safe here for now," Lena said. "Astrid and Beattie are standing watch; we'll do that in pairs. We need to talk about moving, but not right now. We're hungry and exhausted. Whatever we plan will require us to be at a hundred percent. We have to go back for the horses, and we have to figure out where to go." And we need to find a way to take control of our actions. We won't survive if we keep reacting to events.

"And fast," Scott said. "The days as closing in. South or west to the coast."

Beattie slipped back in through the front door and took

her post beside the window. "Astrid will be back in a few. There's no sign of anyone close. Or that anyone has been close. We have time to figure out something smarter than just run."

"They have guns," Tik said.

"We have them at the fort," Beattie said. "They aren't as useful as you think. People tend to rely on them for the wrong reasons. Most shooters don't have the training or talent to hit the side of a skyscraper. It wasn't automatic fire, and every shot gets them closer to no ammo."

"We'll discuss it when Astrid is here," Lena said. "When we have some food in us. A rational plan, not panic."

Tik muttered something and stalked into the kitchen area where Mellow and Siren were preparing stew from the cans and dry goods they'd found. No point in rationing right now.

"Astrid told me she thinks we need to leave the city," Beattie said. "I agree with her. Remember the last encounter with a gang? They are desperate now."

Tik rejoined them. "Nothing has changed. Gangs want to control people. Maybe now it's not through drugs, but food and shelter are pretty powerful levers. Survival is stronger than addiction."

Lena wasn't so sure. Addiction meant getting the next high, and only addicts were a problem. Survival? That was something everyone would kill for, if pressed. "If they are using ammunition, there is a real threat, right?"

"Yeah, so you think someone is resisting?" Scott asked. "Or a rival gang trying to take over?"

Astrid stepped through the door. "It's starting to pour again. I'm pretty sure we're safe for the night."

Would gangsters put up with the weather to take out a handful of potential problems? "Tik? Do you agree?"

"I've been out of it for too long, and the gangs have changed, but I think it would be hard for a boss to keep control if he or she wasted resources like that. Like you said. They're facing a threat of some sort, not just us, even if they know we're here. They'll wait until morning when we have enough light even if it doesn't clear up."

Mellow called out from the kitchen, "Dinner in ten minutes."

"Okay, food, talk, then settle," Lena said. "We make a decision; we plan and then we're done."

DINNER WAS FAR TOO salty for Lena's preference, and still somehow bland. It was also filling, which was the best Lena could hope for. Now they gathered in the living room, with Astrid, Scott, Tik, and Beattie checking for signs of movement outside the windows. The rest on the floor.

"I guess we should start with everyone saying whether they want to stay," Lena said. "You all know how hard the road is no matter which way we go."

"No one wants to stay," Siren said. "I checked already. I still need you all to protect me, so I wanted to understand what my options were."

"Okay, then we go," Scott said. "Tomorrow?"

"We can carefully scavenge one more time," Beattie said, "together, but following my lead. Tomorrow morning. Then we head for the horses. Spend the night in the barn."

"And if we get caught?" Tik asked.

"We won't if you follow my instructions." Beattie glared at him.

"We stick in this area?" Luis asked. "For scavenging? So, we can run for the bridge if we need to?"

The bridge with all its booby traps. Lena kept the

thought to herself, but now she wondered if the traps were set by someone outside Portland to keep the inhabitants in so they can pick them off.

"We might not make the barn before dark," Mellow said. "We should keep the scavenging to a few hours really early in the morning. And to stores, not houses. It looks like this gang is leaving stuff in place so they can shop when they want."

"Good point," Siren said. "But it means the next time they shop in the stores we hit yesterday, they will find out someone is here."

The boy was coming out of his funk, Lena thought. "Okay, so where are we going?"

"South? There are smaller communities downstate," Luis said, "and someone is trading here. So, we go farther than a day's ride before we stop."

"We can't make it far enough south to avoid winter," Scott said. "I suggest we head west. Find a place where we can fish and maybe hunt. Pass the winter and then head south."

"How about we decide when we get to the barn," Luis said. "I'm not sure we have enough energy to plan too far out."

THE MORNING WAS damp but not actually raining. Lena checked the house one more time before they all left. In the two days they'd been here, it had started to feel like a home. But it wasn't, and they would be back on the road by the end of the day. Sleeping in a barn was better than under the stars.

"We head past the market," Beattie said. "There are some smaller stores. We hide and only move when I say it's clear. Don't get separated. Don't make any noise."

She waited until everyone nodded then opened the door, checked the area and slipped through.

Lena brought up the rear just behind Siren. He was the weakest of the team, and her job was to keep him from slowing them down.

They made it to a street of specialty stores without incident. No sounds of fighting in the distance, no signs that anyone else was in the city.

Beattie hurried them through the first door and sent them down the aisles. Nothing was left on the shelves, but it wasn't a food market. Scott came from the back room with a blanket and a handful of baseball caps.

The next store gave up three bags of dried soup mix and a box of instant ramen noodles.

As they crept back into the street, prepared to enter the third store, Beattie held up her hand. The group froze.

"Hey!" The shout came from the end of the road. A man in camo with a rifle pointed in their direction stood in the center of the street. "Found 'em."

52

B eattie shoved Lena to the side and whispered, "Take them home, be careful. Astrid, to me."

Lena knew better than to argue. The man might not know anyone other than Beattie was there. She hated the idea of leaving anyone behind, but the two of them could fight and the rest of the group would be in the way, making them vulnerable.

No sound of firing came as Lena led the remaining six along the side of the store. Luis moved past her to lean out to check if the coast was clear. He ducked back and then motioned for everyone to run across the alley to the next hiding place.

Someone shouted, and then a shot brought the voices to an end. Luis pushed Lena to move because she'd become frozen in fear for the two warriors.

"They will be okay," he whispered. "We need to be at the house when they get back or they'll come looking. More risk, Lena."

She took a breath in and nodded. They ran to join the

group standing in the shadow of a small apartment building.

"If we get separated, keep going for the house," Scott said. "Beattie and Astrid will draw the men away, so we'll have a clear run if we're careful."

"Siren?" Tik asked. "Do we need to worry about you?"

"I'll keep up. Let's go."

It was a nightmare trip alternating between dashing across open spaces and huddling in the shadows, trying not to gasp. Lena kept fighting the urge to run flat out, knowing it would likely expose them to whoever was hunting them.

Luis turned them down the street where they'd left this morning. No one was in sight. "Go." He gave Mellow a little push to start her moving. Everyone followed her, Luis at the rear checking for anyone observing.

Inside the house was exactly the way they'd left it. Lena sagged in relief. They needed a safe place to figure out what to do next. They needed Astrid and Beattie to get back safely, and they needed to escape the city today.

"Did everyone manage to hang on to their bags?" Mellow asked. "I think I'd rather starve on the road than scavenge again."

"Don't get too comfortable," Tik said. "We're out of here as soon as the others return."

"Why didn't we just head over the bridge?" Siren asked. "Or hide in the same building as when we got here? We can't get caught. I know how bad that can be. I got caught when I was a kid. You saw what they did to me."

The scars. So, it was from before Nicolette got her hands on him.

"The bridge is too exposed," Tik said before Lena could answer. "The market building is too close to the action. Probably the first place they'll look."

"Okay, thanks," Siren said. "Good to hear we had a plan."

A quiet knock on the front door alerted them before Astrid opened it enough to slip inside. "Beattie is doing a final pass to check the streets."

"How did you get away?" Mellow asked. "Are you hurt?" She moved to check Astrid for damage and the girl pulled away.

"No problem. They ran off. Scared of two fierce women." Her grin was pure joy. Perhaps her Viking blood was stronger than anyone thought.

"Or going to report to someone," Lena said. "Looking for reinforcements to search for us."

"Yeah, maybe that too," Astrid said. "I like my version better."

It was hard to avoid grinning with her. Lena put her pack down. "We might as well rest until we know what we're doing."

The front door opened, and Beattie pushed a woman through before locking it behind them.

"Found her scoping out the house." She pushed her again into a chair. "Start talking."

"I'm not with the gangs," the woman blurted out. She was clean and healthy, dressed in a dark green slicker and jeans tucked into sturdy hiking boots.

"What's your name?" Lena asked.

"No need for you to know that," she said. "I'm not here to hurt you. I've got an offer."

Beattie pulled out her knife and held it in sight but didn't move closer. "Why should we trust you?"

"You don't have much choice. The gangs will come looking for you now. They don't like strangers taking supplies. We've got a treaty with them. We grow our own, make some stuff, trade at the market."

"Gangs, plural?" Tik asked.

"Two main ones. They can't get to the point where they join up, but they seem happy to work together."

Tik turned to Lena and shook his head. "That won't last. We need to leave. You can't trust a treaty and you can't trust someone who does."

"We can leave," Lena said. "Right now, before they find us."

The woman rolled her eyes. "The bridge is the first place they'll secure. The only way out of here is through Pearl Two. Our place. You go through our back door."

"Tie her up," Lena said. "Don't hurt her. We need to talk, and I don't want her running off."

The kitchen was too close to their guest for a private conversation, so Lena met with everyone on the second floor in the back bedroom. They could observe anyone in the back approach to the house while they talked.

"We don't have a lot of choices," she said. "I don't trust her, or this promise of a safe community in the middle of gang territory."

"She's right about the bridge though," Astrid said. "The people hunting us won't rely on the booby traps. They'll stop us getting close."

"We can't stay here," Siren said. "They will find us eventually. If they're convinced we can't escape, they'll keep looking. And we'll need to be out foraging, and we'll need a fire in the cold weather. There's no way to keep hidden." His voice got tighter the longer he spoke.

"We can check out this Pearl Two place," Luis said. "Play along until we can get to the back door."

It would have to be fast, and the road back to the horses would be farther but safer.

"That woman looks taken care of," Mellow said. "It could be a good deal. A place to wait out the winter."

"And if not, we can all act like we accept their hospitality until we find a chance to run," Tik said.

That wasn't the idea when they left the farm. Lena's vision of a united country was slipping away faster every time they met other people.

53

Jojo, the woman from Pearl Two, led them through a series of streets before stopping in the lobby of an old hotel.

"The tunnels are a bit shaky, but no gangs know how to get down here. We closed off the old tourist entrances and made a few new ones. You'll be blindfolded until we're in."

"No," Lena said. "If you don't trust us, we'll stay above ground."

"Too dangerous. It's only for a couple of minutes," Jojo said. "Look, what if I take one of you, blindfolded, in and back to confirm it's doable."

Doable wasn't Lena's worry, she didn't trust Jojo at all.

"Let Siren go," Scott said. "He can tell us what happens, and we can decide then."

"Why do I feel dispensable?" Siren asked. "I'll do it." He stepped forward and Jojo pulled a black cloth from her jacket.

"We'll be back soon," she said before leading Siren

through a door in the side that still had an "authorized access only" sign attached.

"I get the feeling we're close," Beattie said. "You can't blame her for being cautious, but I'm going first if Siren sets our minds at ease. Astrid last."

"Leaving a fighter on each end," Tik said. "Good idea. I'll go in the middle."

They sorted out the order to ensure they would have protection at both ends of the transition.

"Should we try to figure it out?" Astrid asked. "The path? Like if we need to escape?"

"We don't want to come back this way," Luis said. "The gangs don't have enough to occupy their time. I'm pretty sure they'll continue to hunt us until some other distraction comes along."

Jojo had assured them that they weren't committed to staying in Pearl Two, but Lena's experience had her planning escape routes for every step of the way.

"It's fine," Siren said. "Jojo got me disoriented right away and then we went into an old street after a short flight of steps."

"Okay," Beattie said. "Me first."

It only took minutes for Lena to be standing in front of an old saloon. The only source of light was the flashlight Siren held. On the edges of the tunnel walls, there was evidence of damage, but the whole area had an aura of abandonment. They would move fast down here and maybe inside this supposedly safe community.

"Okay, follow me," Jojo said as she led Astrid into the space. "We'll need to cross a couple of intersections when we get out. And you'll leave blindfolded, too. We don't want to lose this passage because someone blabbed."

Despite being spun around before entering, Lena had

the impression they were headed in the same direction as they'd followed above ground. Portland wasn't a big city, so they would only be safe here for a short while.

The air was damp and stuffy, but the path was clear. Jojo led them at a jog for long enough to make Lena long for a rest and then came to an abrupt stop.

"We exit here. It's going to take longer to take you out because the exit is a bit rougher. I can take two of you at a time if you want."

Lena considered the risk. If they were close and safe, getting into Pearl Two was critical, and Jojo wasn't about to put them in danger after bringing them so far. She checked with Beattie, who nodded.

"Beattie and Siren," Lena said. "How long will you be?"

"You got a watch to time me?" Jojo asked as she tied the first blindfold.

"Just give us an idea," Scott said. "It's hard to wait down here in the dark."

"Look, maybe five minutes, maybe ten. I got to make sure the place I leave you is secure. It's also out of sight of the entrance, so we might get a bit detoured if the street isn't empty."

So, the whole idea of it being safer to take the tunnel was bull. "Be as fast as you can," Lena said.

Lena wondered what Jojo was doing as each pair went with her. The time between was not regular, sometimes it was around a count of three hundred and sometimes five. The last trip, to take her and Astrid, still hadn't started after a count of six hundred. If the streets were not safe, then would Jojo keep trying to move them through up top?

"More likely to confuse us," Astrid said when Lena mentioned it. "If we compare timing, we'll never guess how far we had to go."

"Okay, let's go." Jojo stepped in from the corridor and tossed the blindfolds to Lena and Astrid.

How long had she been listening?

Jojo grabbed Lena's arm and dragged her forward. As soon as they stepped inside the new corridor, she spun Lena twice in one direction and twice in the other. The disorientation worked because Lena would have sworn she was going to hit the wall when Jojo told her to walk.

It didn't take long for them to arrive. Jojo said it was safe to remove the blindfolds. Lena blinked at the brightness and looked around. Another hotel lobby, but a lower-end version. They'd come to the edges of the city, as expected.

"Stay here," Jojo said. "I'll scout and be back in a few. Then we'll head out."

She slipped away, and Beattie moved to the door to keep an eye on the street.

"We could go," Siren said. "There must be another way out now we're so far from the bridge."

"Why would we go now?" Mellow asked.

"I need to tell Nicolette what's happening. I have to go back to her."

The boy's eyes were wide with fear. Lena wondered what changed his mind about Pearl Two. Then she heard shots in the distance.

"We make that decision when we know more," Lena said. "And we're not going back to Live Right. We're keeping to our plan. South, then back east. You can go alone or just be patient."

Jojo slipped back through the door, panting. "It's not clear. I have to go deal with something."

"And us?" Beattie asked, taking a step toward Jojo. "We just wait here to be attacked?"

Jojo put her hand on the knife in her belt. "Step back."

Beattie stared her down for a few seconds then moved one step away. "Well?"

"No. The gates to Pearl Two are only a few blocks away. I give you directions. You wait until I'm gone for a count of two hundred and make your way, if it's safe. Don't come to help me. This is my skillset, and it won't help if I have a bunch of strangers with me when the gang is looking for the people who stole from them."

She waited until Beattie stepped farther back.

"Okay. Out this door and turn right at the intersection. There's a big fence a block away. Follow it until you get to the gates."

Jojo pushed the door open and left.

54

"We can't stay here," Astrid said.

Every time they thought leaving was a good idea, shots sounded. Lena wasn't willing to lose anyone this close to safety. She wasn't willing to lose anyone ever.

"She's right," Beattie said. "We need it to be daylight when we head for this Pearl Two place. It's going to be dark in a couple of hours. The fighting isn't close, and Jojo said we were only a block or two away from the gate."

Not exactly what was said, but surely Jojo brought them close enough. "We stay together." She said it as an order. Beattie and Astrid might be their protectors, but Lena wasn't going to let them take risks.

"Yes," Astrid said. "I'll go in front, check to make sure the way is clear, or make it clear if I need to. Beattie keeps our rear safe."

"I'll stick with Astrid," Tik said. "Everyone ready?"

The others stood and shouldered their packs. Getting into what was becoming their normal order: Tik and Astrid at the front, Mellow and Scott, then Siren and Lena with Beattie stepping into the last place.

"Are you okay with Astrid's plan?" Lena asked Beattie.

"We talked it through. It doesn't really matter if I lead or follow. She's grown a lot in a short amount of time."

"You've been a good influence," Lena said. "I don't know how you did it."

"She likes me," Beattie said with a grin. "She doesn't see me as an authority figure. She listens."

Lena had seen how Astrid stuck close to Beattie. There was more to their relationship than just 'like'. But they weren't in middle grade, and it was none of her business because Astrid was well able to take care of herself. "Okay."

"I'm going to check the street," Astrid said. "Two seconds, don't follow me."

She stepped through the door without waiting for any response. It was more than two seconds, but she joined them quickly. "Okay, I saw the fence, and we're clear that far. There's no cover when we reach it, so stick as close as you can."

When they got to the fence, Lena pressed herself into the metal and held her breath, trying to sense if anyone was near them. It all felt really still. Not peaceful, more like that moment in a horror movie when you know something bad is about to happen but you can't stop it.

"Tik and I will head to the next intersection," Astrid said. "We'll stay in sight. Wait for our signal before you come. Come fast."

She led Tik along the wall at a crouch. Lena touched Siren's shoulder as he leaned out to check on them. "Don't move. We'll get the signal."

"It's clear," Scott whispered and then took off at a crouching run.

They stopped and Astrid motioned for them to stay down. The buildings were not hotels and small businesses. There were a few low-rise apartment buildings and more single houses. The wall continued without break as far as Lena could see. Three, maybe four blocks and she could see no sign of anything resembling a gate.

"I think Jojo lied," she whispered to Beattie. "We should look for a place to hide for the night. Maybe we can keep going in the morning. Find a way out?"

"I don't think we'll make it," Beattie said. "If I'm right, that direction will dump us in the river, another bridge that could be watched. We need to go through Pearl Two, that's the coast side."

"Shut up," Astrid hissed.

Shots sounded from their right.

"We're going to get killed," Siren whispered.

"No," Astrid said. "I'm going to find out where they are and deal with it. You keep heading along the wall."

Beattie ran past Lena and grabbed Astrid. "You will not go alone."

Astrid pulled away and ran toward the noise of a fight. Beattie swore and followed her. It all happened so fast; Lena couldn't stop them leaving.

"No way are we getting separated," she said. "Get across. We need to keep them in sight."

The street opposite was all single-family homes in the same style. Two-story, front garden, gray siding and roofs. The two fighters had headed through the alley. By the time the rest of the group were safely hiding behind a large rhododendron bush, they only saw Beattie as she turned onto the next street.

"We can't just keep running," Tik said. "They think we're headed for safety."

"You and me," Lena said. "Everyone else stay here. We know where you are."

Tik handed his pack to Scott. "Leave yours here," he said to Lena. "Bring a crossbow and some bolts. If we're going, we need to be armed."

Within seconds, Lena was running beside Tik down the street where Beattie disappeared. They tried to keep to the cover of trees, but it slowed them down.

Up ahead she saw Astrid standing alone, her crossbow aimed at something out of sight down another street. No sign of Beattie.

Tik led her closer along the fence line where shrubs had gone wild growing unattended. Not perfect cover, but definitely better than nothing.

"Back off!" Astrid's shout was boiling with fury.

Lena took the last steps to the edge of the fence. Blood smeared Astrid's face. Her bow didn't waver.

"I said back off," she repeated, then shot a single bolt.

Someone cursed. Close enough to be a danger. Lena heard running, and Astrid didn't rearm.

Beattie careened around the corner and past them. Astrid followed. "Get the fuck up and come with us," she said.

No one came from the street to answer the attack. Tik pulled Lena's arm and ran with her.

They rejoined the others at the bush. "What happened?"

Beattie was checking Astrid for injuries, both out of breath.

"Two guys tried to attack," Astrid gasped. "They were hiding, ready to ambush us."

"I took one out. We ran, but the other guy caught me. Astrid wouldn't go. The bolt got him in the shoulder. He'll be after us soon."

"Back to the wall," Tik said. "Forget stealth, we move fast and we find that gate."

"The guy who grabbed me said something," Beattie told Lena. "He said 'she'll be happy we got them'."

"The gang is run by a woman? Why am I shocked by that?"

55

I t turned out that the gate was just a sliding panel in the wall. Not secret, but defensible. The panel slid aside as they reached it, and they were pulled inside. Now they were sitting in the living room of a house that sat directly behind the gate. Alone, with no idea what they were supposed to do.

"They were ready for us," Tik said. "They were watching. And if it was from the top of the wall, they saw us run."

"We can get answers later," Lena said. "Job one is to... I don't know, meet the leader, be accepted? Figure out what we're going to do."

"They can't all be job one," Siren said. "Be careful what you say, I think we're being observed."

"We're being guarded." Mellow moved from one window to the next. "The place actually looks occupied. I can see three more houses here. All have vegetable gardens in front, maybe in back, too. Curtains, toys. This place is well protected."

Beattie leaned out to look through the kitchen. "Clean. There's a pot on the stove, but nothing cooking. In the back, yeah. Vegetables, but this late, most of the harvest is done."

"So, what do we think?" Mellow asked. "Are we going to stay, or not?"

"It won't be up to us," Lena said. "I'm hoping we can take a few days to decide. After what we just went through, my gut is telling me to run out of here as fast as we can."

"This place is peaceful and productive," Siren said. "Why wouldn't we stay, if they let us?"

This place was too peaceful and productive given what was outside the walls. "How do they keep it that way?" Lena asked. "If the gangs rule everything outside, why haven't they taken over in here? The wall is strong, but there must be weak points."

Beattie sat on the end of the sofa. "If they have enough people to watch for attacks, it would be relatively easy to defend. People will fight for safety. They would before, but now? It's harder to find and more precious for it."

"I'm with Lena," Luis said. "Whatever the rest of you decide, I'm not sticking around unless someone has a good explanation for all this."

"You think whoever is running the place has made a deal? With the gang leader? Or someone else?" Tik paced the room as if he could walk away from his doubts.

"They trade with them. At the market," Astrid said. "If they grow enough food, that makes them valuable. Protection from the gangs for the price of fresh vegetables and whatever else they have in here?"

That didn't seem enough of a deal. Lena could understand the gang leader, whoever she was, seeing the value. But whoever ran this place? Protection from the people who were the problem from the same people causing it? Like an old-fashioned protection racket?

"We don't know what price we'll have to pay," she said. "Some of us have been through this before. You work for your shelter, but you can't ever get even. I'm saying we need to know more, and we need some rest."

"Did women run other gangs, Tik?" Beattie asked. "Those men definitely report to a woman."

Tik looked up from where he was staring out the window. "Not for long, or not obviously. I guess who we thought was a leader could be a figurehead. But gangs are made up of men who don't like taking orders from women."

"Because they don't think women can be criminals?" Astrid asked.

"Yeah. Men who respect women don't generally end up in gangs. Maybe in the old days, but not now. If they said a woman was running the gang, then she'd be mean and violent. She wouldn't hold their loyalty otherwise."

Lena thought back to Abigail and her Community of Truth. On their way from New Surrey to the farm, she'd trapped people by offering them shelter for work. Escaping her cost them their supplies and almost killed them by the time they arrived at the farm. Abigail was certain she was doing the right thing for her people.

"Women are just as capable of running a gang as men," she said, "but Tik is right. It would be from behind a man."

"If they let us take a few days to decide, we could clean up," Siren said. "Wash our clothes. Maybe get a haircut? I'm so tired of looking and feeling dirty."

As much as Lena wanted to tell Siren to stop complaining, the thought of a bath made her realize how filthy they really were. The last time she'd felt human was at Fort Revelation.

56

"We're in the process of canning, pickling, and salting." A woman had joined them without anyone noticing. Had she been in the house already?

She was in her fifties, dressed like she lived in that era, too. Red bandana holding back blond curls. Jean shirt tied at her waist, jeans with folded cuffs, black oxford shoes.

"Good to meet you folks," she said, glancing around the room. "Jojo said you'd make it."

"Are you in charge?" Lena asked.

"Trixie Shine." She held out her hand to shake.

"Lena Custordin." Lena shook her hand and introduced the others. "We need a safe place to stay for the winter, or a way out of town."

"Direct. I like that. We can always use some help. If you want to contribute, we can talk about staying a while."

"How big is this place?" Astrid asked. "I mean, with those gangs outside, how do you keep people safe?"

"We have stout walls and pretty much everything we need inside them," Trixie answered. "Why don't we take a bit of a tour when you've had a chance to ask your questions?"

A tour of the best parts, Lena thought, or maybe just the closest. She tried to put Abigail in the past, but the memory kept intruding. "Like I said, we don't know if we want to stay, but if we do, it'll be just for the winter. What are the terms?"

Trixie put her hands on her hips and glared at Lena. "Look, honey, you seem to think it's up to you. We let you in, you passed that test, but we don't just let anyone stick around. You contribute or you leave."

"You left us out there on purpose?" Tik asked. "To be slaughtered?"

"It's not like that. We need to make sure anyone who gets in the door is capable of taking care of themselves. You did, and no one got hurt. If you don't like my methods, you can leave. We don't have any burning need for skills."

Pissing her off wasn't going to help them make a decision. In fact, Trixie seemed eager to have them leave. Lena put her hand on Tik's arm to get his attention and the shook her head. She turned to Trixie. "I think we started off wrong," she said. "We are not looking for a permanent home, but we have every intention of working if we all agree it's a good place to wait out the winter."

"What skills?" Trixie asked, not bending from her antagonistic stance.

"Two soldiers, a medic, the rest of us are able to do all kinds of things. No one is looking for a free ride. We've all run into places that looked great at first. We're anxious to make sure we don't get trapped. Been there before."

Trixie removed her hands from her hips and smiled. "I guess I've been inside the walls too long. I forget the world is still healing, people who take power don't always make good decisions. This a free community. We support each other and we do more than survive. No one is forced to stay. You don't incur debt as long as you do your job. Stay the winter and leave when you are ready."

Like she was going to tell them it was a trap, Lena thought. "How did you build this place? The walls weren't here before, right?"

"Sit," Trixie said. "Annie, bring some refreshments."

A young girl came in carrying a tray loaded with pastries and tea. She passed out the cups and offered cream and sugar, then placed the plate with treats on the ottoman before returning to the kitchen.

"Mostly this was a hipster area," Trixie said. "They had a bunch of what you might call cottage industries. Bakeries, small farms in joined-up backyards. A bunch of chickens, goats, and sheep. A shed where they turned fleece into yarn. A butcher. Probably not completely authorized. They are a godsend now. And we gathered the metal for the walls early on. We had a blacksmith. He's moved on, but he trained a few apprentices."

"How many people live here?" Mellow asked. "What happens if some one gets sick, or injured?"

"A couple of thousand," Trixie said. "We have some doctors, but the big sicknesses like cancer or diabetes are deadly. The world is a long way from being able to deal with that stuff again. We accept it. You the doctor in this group?"

"Nothing complicated, natural cures and things," Mellow said.

"Can always use a fresh mind on healing," Trixie said. "And we need strong backs. Got a foundry to repair. Then we can make all kinds of stuff to trade. Maybe hire some mercenaries to clean up the rest of the city, make it safe to walk around again. The boy is hurt?"

"I can still contribute," Siren said. "Just not hard labor."

Trixie gave him a warm smile. "No problem, sweetie, we have plenty of jobs you can do."

"If we want to stay, it will be the whole group," Lena said. "Are we allowed to stay together?"

"Plenty of empty houses. If that works for you, no one will complain."

It seemed too good. They'd fought so hard to get here, Lena couldn't believe everything was going to be so simple. "We need to talk in private," she said.

"This house is set up for temporary visitors. You can shower, not an unending supply of hot water, but should be enough. We'll send over dinner. Leave your dirty clothes on the porch and they'll be laundered. You have until tomorrow lunch to decide if you want to ask for shelter or directions."

She stood and walked through the kitchen to say something to whoever was in there, then the back door closed.

Beattie stepped into the other room and confirmed they were alone. She locked the back door and then did the same to the front.

"Let's clean up," Luis said, "then we should have some time to poke around before bed. I need to see for myself that people are okay. And, Lena, I know you meant well, but I think I'll be making my own decision about staying."

57

"We'll need to bring the horses," Astrid said. "There must be a way to get in and out without going through the city."

"We'll ask," Lena said. "If not, someone should go and set them free. I hate to lose them, but parading our horses through a gang-controlled city is a crazy risk."

"They had a stable," Scott said. "Must be a way."

They had discussed their options last night before bed. The decision was to stay until they could head south in the new year. And to leave as early as sensible, rather than risk another rush to shelter next winter. There were still things to be talked through, but now it was up to Trixie to decide. If she didn't want them, or all of them, they would leave, retrieve the horses and go to the coast. Another choice that was really out of their hands.

"I'll take care of the horses," Luis said. "I understand that everyone is happy, the place seems safe, but I'm not sticking it out here. It's too organized, I'm not going to be happy, and that likely means trouble. I'll bring the horses to the south.

Somewhere safe near the I-5. You come find me when you leave."

Lena had wondered what Luis would do. He'd avoided going into the cult with them, thank goodness. But like he said, Pearl Two seemed safe and productive. A place Lena would love to bring into an alliance in the future. No one was walking around in a blissful daze, people looked like people, not beautiful runway models.

"Is there something we're missing?" Beattie asked. "I ranged pretty far last night. No red flags."

Luis shook his head. "Nothing but my experience. I guess I've been on the road too long. Settling here is a bit like giving up. If I only have the horses to look after, it will be easy to find a place to hole up. I'll leave some markers so you can find me. Seems smart to have someone on the outside if things go wrong."

As much as Lena hoped they were right about this community, Luis had a point. And having the horses outside meant they didn't have to account for stabling and food in their earnings. Lena wanted to build up a stock of supplies before they left for the south. This time she wasn't going to be stuck foraging because they ran out of grains or protein. At least until they got somewhere that game was more plentiful.

"Okay," she said. "We'll walk you to the exit. It will give us a chance to see how people get in and out. I want to make sure you aren't just shoved out the front to race a gang member to the bridge."

Someone turned the handle of the front door, but it was locked.

Lena opened the door to find Trixie waiting, and a sack full of their clothes leaning against the wall.

"You made your decision?" Trixie asked.

"Yes. Come in." Lena hefted the sack of clothes into the living room before sitting on the couch next to Trixie. "Thanks for last night," she said. "It's been a while since we've been able to be really clean."

"We forget what a luxury it is," Trixie said. She pulled a flowered silk scarf, possibly Hermes, out of her pocket. "Found this for Siren. People will know he's hurt right away and cut him some slack. So, what are we dealing with? You want to stick around?"

"If you let us," Lena said. "Luis will leave, but the rest of us want to stay and work until spring."

"I asked around and my folks are happy if you stay," Trixie said. "We'll get you set up with a couple of houses. Assign you work, and a few guides for the first week because you need to be oriented. There's a few rules they'll tell you about, mostly if you don't cause problems, you'll be fine. You leave anything outside?"

"No," Luis said. "If you can have someone show me out the back door, I'll take off today."

They'd agreed to keep the horses a secret, and the fact that Luis was hanging around. The group still held a thick and undefined sense of suspicion about Pearl Two, so the secrets seemed like a lifeline until they could be sure it was paranoia, not instinct.

"Okay then," Trixie said. "You'll be here tonight, as guests, don't worry about jobs. Tomorrow, you move and start working. I'll send two guards to escort you, Luis, to the back door as you call it." She stood and said some words of welcome, and then left them.

"I'd like to go with Luis," Siren said. "Oh, don't panic. I meant to the exit. Not outside. I want to know more about the area. Try to find something I'd be good at that isn't hard physical work."

"We might not have a choice of jobs," Mellow said. "She knows you're still healing, and she seems to like you. I'm sure Trixie will find you some appropriate work."

"Grab your stuff and get ready for our move," Lena said. "If we have two houses, we'll need to think about splitting up. And I think we'll all go say goodbye to Luis at the exit. Just in case."

58

"We keep together," Lena said as they walked toward the house designated as a town hall.

A man had been waiting in the guest house living room when they came down for breakfast. He assured them that permanent housing would be theirs, and unless an emergency came up, this was the last time someone would enter uninvited.

The two houses they were to call home were side by side, three bedrooms in each and a gate in the fence between them. Lena and Scott shared the first house with Tik and Mellow. The second one held Astrid, Beattie, and Siren. It felt a bit like the grown-ups were together, and the kids had their own space. But it worked. Now she wanted it to be clear that the group was not going to split.

"Should we eat together? Dinner, I mean?" Astrid asked. "Like, we won't know our shifts, but we need to talk about what we see, right?"

It seemed everyone had lingering doubts about Pearl Two.

"That's a good idea," Tik said. "I don't want to find out by accident that someone is missing. And when it's time to leave, we all need to coordinate."

"It's going to be months," Siren said. "Why are we talking about leaving?"

"You want to stay?" Astrid asked. "The road isn't comfortable, right?"

The antagonism between them ebbed and flowed. Lena hoped it was some form of teenage rivalry and would disappear as the two got older. "If you want to stay when we're ready to leave, then you can. That goes for everyone. Just let us know."

"I can't," Siren said. "Nicolette gave me a job. I have to do as she asked."

Not the best motivation to spend months on the road with all the challenges. But it went a long way toward explaining his moods. "Like you said, we have months," she said. "Let's find out what Trixie thinks we should do to contribute before we do anything else." Lena already had plans to prepare for their departure. Supplies, knowledge, timing.

THE TOWN HALL was just another house like their lodging. The area was pretty consistent in design; no large houses jammed into small lots like other communities before the plagues. This one had been modified by taking out walls, providing an open plan that allowed for meetings. Trixie waited for them at a desk covered in paperwork. She looked up from an open ledger and motioned for them to take seats.

"I have your assignments," she said. "We'll assess your performance and make changes if we need to. It's all for the benefit of the community, the right people in the right jobs."

"Do we have a say?" Scott asked. "I mean, we know our skills better than you, and you know what the community needs. We can make the right choices now rather than move us around."

"I make the decisions," Trixie said, "you do the work. Your guide will report on you. You get a voice when you commit to us. Are you ready to do that, or are you still just passing through?"

"Maybe we should hear you out," Lena said. "We're here to work and then go. If that changes, someone will tell you."

Trixie nodded. "Good. It sounds like you give people choices. Okay. Mellow, you head over to the medical wards. I'll send an escort. You'll work from ten through to dinner unless we need you to go longer." She held out a box of watches. "Keep them wound. We run on set schedules."

Lena put the watch on her wrist. A Rolex. The others she could see were luxury brands, Patek Philippe, TAG Heuer, and Audemars Piguet.

"Astrid and Beattie, you join the guards. Your unit leader will assign your shift."

So far, Trixie had it right, but those were the easy ones.

"Lena, we have a couple of classes of teenagers. You'll join the teachers. You'll teach what we say, right?"

"I'm used to following a curriculum. Anything special about yours?"

"Basics. Mostly prep for jobs we have here." Trixie watched Lena as if waiting for a protest.

"Sounds smart," Lena said. "I assume someone will be there to orient me?"

"Yep. So now we have three men, or two men and a boy," Trixie said. "Scott and Tik, you head off to the foundry. We need strong backs to clear it and then start repairs. Siren, start in the pantry work, we always need dishwashers. I'll see how you do with that and then maybe I can find something more... appropriate."

Two men walked in from the street. Both dressed in plaid shirts and jeans, both with beards and hair caught into a bun. The hipster look seemed to be a uniform. "These are your guides. Brent will take the men; Ramon will take the women. I'll get a report today on your abilities. If we need to reassign someone, I'll send a message."

Trixie turned back to her ledger, dismissing them.

DINNER THAT NIGHT was a pork stew delivered by one of Lena's students. The boy told her they would be able to buy their own groceries after a couple of days' work. "You can still have us cook for you. Just let us know the night before."

"We need to look into prices and wages," Scott said. "I don't like not knowing."

"I'll see what I can find out," Lena said. "I have more free time with the school schedule."

"I can ask too," Mellow said. "We don't have many patients. Everyone seems pretty healthy."

"Anything that keeps us out of any kind of obligation is good," Tik said. "We might have something to share already."

"What do you mean by something?" Beattie asked.

"Something to explain our suspicions," Scott said. "We worked the foundry. It's a long way from being productive, but we stumbled over a bunch of die casts today. For weapons."

"So not just pots, pans, and bolts." Beattie pushed her empty bowl to the center of the table. "They still need ammunition."

"There's a metal punch too," Tik said. "Bullet casings. They just need to add the primer."

"How did the other workers react?" Lena asked.

"Like it was just another day on the job," Tik said. "Trixie knows something about what they produced in that place before. The equipment I saw today didn't need repairing, just cleaning up. Still a big job, and she doesn't have supplies like metal to be melted down, but there's something going on."

"Maybe she needs weapons for the guards," Astrid said. "We patrolled the fence today, but they said we'd be going outside to deal with the gangs before too long."

"Guess we keep our eyes open and our mouths shut," Lena said. "Make it to spring so we can leave."

59

Nothing overt happened in the two months following their arrival to Pearl Two. Nothing to settle their minds, nothing to prove their suspicions. Now, on New Year's Eve, Lena sat at the table with the others, drinking cider and waiting for the sun to set.

"Luis is fine," Astrid said. "We took him some of the stuff we've saved. The blankets and water skins. And the rice and beans. He says we should be able to get going early."

Astrid and Beattie had visited Luis every couple of weeks since they'd been given permission to explore the area. Knowing where he was helped Lena plan and gave them a secure place to store her supplies. The winter weather was mild, but she didn't know if that was normal or not. Risking an early departure was dangerous. Being stuck in a snowstorm on the road could mean death even a couple of weeks' travel south.

"We could move down to him," Beattie said. "It's not as comfortable as here, but there is room."

"Not yet," Lena said. "But it's a good idea. The closer we are to leaving, the more I worry Trixie will stop us."

"She isn't planning anything," Siren said. "I work with her every day. She's not a bad person, and I wish you would all accept that. Look at what she gave me." He gestured to his clothing. All designer brands.

The contents of the upscale stores were never about survival. And Trixie soon realized Siren could be motivated with gifts. He'd come home with a little trinket or accessory every day.

Siren's history with the cult didn't give Lena much confidence in his ability to recognize a schemer. "Why did she move you from the kitchens to her office?"

"She said it was best for the community. I have skills she needs." His words were defensive. He had no idea and was parroting Trixie.

"It's nice to be together tonight," Mellow said. "It's been a while since our shifts lined up like this. I miss what's going on. How is the foundry doing?"

Scott looked at Tik before answering. Were they keeping secrets? Then, after both glancing at Siren, Scott said, "It's almost set up. I'm not sure what our assignment will be in a week. But still no materials. Maybe it's just being kept a secret. I get the sense the people working there are on a need-to-know standing. Someone doesn't trust us with the truth."

Someone? Trixie. If she was planning to build an armory, she would keep the plans close. The community was big enough that there had to be some spies in with the population. Three groups had arrived after Lena's, and every one of them could have ulterior motives. The gangs outside the wall were pushing for more food and clothing than Trixie handed out at the markets. Outlying communities were likely running into hard times and looking for shelter they could take.

"Some guys came in today," Siren said. It was like he could hear her thoughts. "From up north. Vancouver, in Canada."

A long way to come in the winter. Lena wondered if they would talk about how things were going up north. "How did they get here?" Lena asked. "Did Trixie put them up in the guest house?"

"Came by boat," Siren said. "No. She let them stay in her place. I think they were traders. She knew them. Called them by name right away, Ben and Zeke."

A trade group? Suddenly, the work in Pearl Two started to make sense. If Trixie was trading with other cities, then whatever they made in the foundry would be worth more than a few hand-woven blankets.

"Maybe that's where the raw material is coming from," she said.

"They told her the other merchandise was on the boat," Siren said. "Not like they were planning to bring it here. More like they expected Trixie to hand over stuff."

"Did you find anything in the records?" Lena asked. "An inventory of trade materials? An agreement?"

"I don't get to see that stuff," Siren said. "Why?"

"I'm not sure what kind of trade goods would be worth traveling here. Even in a boat, bad weather will be a problem. And if it's a trade, why didn't they bring their side of it from the boat?"

Siren shrugged. "Maybe their part is in the summer, like we provide what they need at this time of the year, and they bring down stuff we need in the summer. I can try to find out. Trixie told me I was going to work with them a bit."

He was still the weakest link in the group. Too slight to do manual labor, although he'd never be strong enough without working at it, and he was too willing to take things at face value to be useful in any shady plans.

Just another thing to worry about. Lena promised herself she would get to know these new people before Siren was in too deep with them. He wouldn't betray them on purpose, but an idle comment could be just as damaging.

"Let's just celebrate," Mellow said. "It's a whole new year and we'll be on the road soon, exploring the world."

WANT MORE?

If you enjoyed reading The Foundry please consider helping other readers to find the story by leaving a review.

FREE EBOOK

Claim your copy of A Choice to Make when you sign up for my newsletter and get a glimpse of Lena and Brian at the end of the plagues.

ALSO BY PA WILSON

For more books by P A Wilson

Use the QR code below or go to pawilson.ca

ACKNOWLEDGMENTS

People think that the process of writing is solitary. That's not the case for me. I have help from so many people it would be hard to acknowledge everyone, but I'll give it a try.

The support and inspiration I get from my writer's groups is incalculable. The Vancouver Writers Social Group opens my mind to other ways of telling a story. The Royal City Literary Arts Society gives me the opportunity to meet and share with other writers who have more knowledge than I do. The Other 11 Months group is where I learn about getting the words on the page. And my critique group who helps me find the best parts of the story I want to tell. Thanks to all of the members of these great groups.

Last of all, but definitely a huge part of the process, my beta readers. These are the people who love stories and are willing, and more than able, to tell me if my finished story is ready for you, my readers.

ABOUT THE AUTHOR

Perry Wilson is a Canadian author based in Vancouver, BC who has big ideas and an itch to tell stories. Having spent some time on university, a career, and life in general, she returned to writing in 2008 and hasn't looked back since (well, maybe a little, but only while parallel parking).

She is a member of the Vancouver Writers Social Group, The Royal City Literary Arts Society, and The Surrey Writing Workshop. Perry has self-published several novels. She writes the Madeline Journeys, a fantasy series about a high-powered lawyer who finds herself trapped in a magical world, the Quinn Larson Quests, which follows the adventures of a wizard named Quinn who must contend with volatile fae in the heart of Vancouver, and the Charity Deacon Investigations, a mystery thriller series about a private eye who tends to fall into serious trouble with her cases, and The Riverton Romances, a series based in a small town in Oregon, one of her favorite states. Her stand-alone novels are Breaking the Bonds, Closing the Circle, and The Dragon at The Edge of The Map.

For more information
www.pawilson.ca
pawilson@pawilson.ca